A LITTLE LIGHT MISCHIEF

By Cat Sebastian

The Turner Series
The Soldier's Scoundrel
The Lawrence Browne Affair
The Ruin of a Rake
A Little Light Mischief (novella)

The Seducing the Sedgwicks Series
It Takes Two to Tumble
A Gentleman Never Keeps Score

The Regency Impostors Series
Unmasked by the Marquess
A Duke in Disguise

COMING SOON
The Duchess Deception

A Little Light Mischief

A Turner Novella

Cat Sebastian

AVONIMPULSE
An Imprint of HarperCollinsPublishers

Excerpt from *A Duke in Disguise* copyright © 2019 by Cat Sebastian

Digital Edition AUGUST 2019 ISBN: 978-0-06-295103-8
Print Edition ISBN: 978-0-06-295104-5

Cover design by Patricia Barrows
Cover illustration by Frederika Ribes
Cover photographs © Jenn LeBlanc / Illustrated Romance

Avon Impulse and the Avon Impulse logo are registered trademarks of HarperCollins Publishers in the United States of America.

Avon and HarperCollins are registered trademarks of HarperCollins Publishers in the United States of America and other countries.

FIRST EDITION

19 20 21 22 23   HDC   10 9 8 7 6 5 4 3 2 1

ACKNOWLEDGMENTS

As always, I'm grateful for the support of my agent, Deidre Knight. This book would not have seen the light of day without the guidance and enthusiasm of my editor, Elle Keck. Many thanks to everyone at Avon, especially the art department for creating a cover that makes my heart grow three sizes every time I look at it. And yet more thanks to Margrethe Martin and Michele Howe, who read and offered feedback on an early version of this novella.

A LITTLE LIGHT MISCHIEF

CHAPTER ONE

London, January 1818

Alice had her eye on that lady's maid.

Most lady's maids Alice had met were either French or at least pretended to be French; failing that, they were English-women of the austere, rail-thin variety. Molly Wilkins was neither, and Alice didn't know how she was supposed to concentrate on her sewing—or whatever it was she was meant to be doing—when there was an ample bosom or a pert backside within reach at all moments.

Not that there was much of anything to do. Alice had never been so idle in her life. Some lady's companions were little more than unpaid drudges, and that was the fate she had gladly anticipated when Mrs. Wraxhall rescued her from the vicarage; it had been the only kind of life she had ever known. But no, Mrs. Wraxhall didn't need an extra set of hands to help with the mending or settle matters of domestic diplomacy among the staff. She had servants for those tasks, as well as for tasks Alice hadn't even known existed before arriving in London, such as packing gowns between layers of tissue paper, which Molly was doing presently.

When Alice had ventured to ask her benefactress in what small ways she could be of use, Mrs. Wraxhall had waved an airy hand and said, "Simply adorn the drawing room, my dear." Alice had to bite the inside of her cheek so she didn't laugh herself into a stupor; she had never adorned a blessed thing in her life, and at twenty-eight wasn't apt to start now. So she hid in the sewing room, away from Mrs. Wraxhall's callers, and amused herself with the most useless stitchery she had ever done in her life.

If it weren't for the not-so-small matter of Molly Wilkins's bosom and the absolute conviction that the lady's maid was up to no good, Alice thought she could be quite content in Mrs. Wraxhall's household. Well, as long as she stayed in the sewing room.

She tore her gaze from the maid and bent over her embroidery. Her silks were in a frightful tangle, possibly because she had spent most of the morning distracted by Molly's packing of Mrs. Wraxhall's trunks and hadn't properly attended to her own work. Not that embroidering handkerchiefs with flowers and fairies and all manner of silliness counted as work—it was just a way to fill the hours in between meals and sleep, a way to use hands that had spent decades at another's service.

The crux of the matter was that every time Molly leaned

over the trunk, her fichu came untucked, giving Alice an eyeful of creamy breasts. And when she tried to tuck her scarf back in, as she was this very minute, much to Alice's consternation, she made a great show of patting herself down and rearranging the contents of her bodice. Alice tried to tell herself that it was the coarseness of the girl's behavior that had drawn her attention, but found she couldn't sustain the lie. That was another problem with idleness—there was nothing to distract her from the unwanted thoughts that flitted in and out of her mind.

"Oh, drat," Alice said in frustration, realizing she must have dropped her needle while gawping at this latest episode of tucking and self-groping.

"Let me get it, miss," Molly said with her emphatically not-French accent, falling to her knees on the carpet. Alice struggled to find a place to look that wasn't Molly's backside. "Here it is!" Molly held up the needle, smiling in that lazy, crooked way she had. She had a gap between her top teeth that gave her a faintly rakish air and a crinkling around her eyes that made it impossible to guess her age. Only a few years younger than Alice herself, she reckoned, but Alice felt withered and dry in comparison.

Alice's hands clenched around the edges of her embroidery hoop. "Thank you," she managed, her voice sounding rusty with disuse.

Instead of handing the needle directly to Alice, Molly slid it into the edge of Alice's work. It felt impertinent, this practiced gesture. Too familiar. As if they were friends, as if Alice had the capacity for anything like friendship. Alice wasn't made for that; she was made for more practical things like lending a hand on washing day, or persuading the butcher to wait another month for payment—all the stretching and scraping that went into making things right for her father. Even this fanciful embroidery wasn't what Alice's hands were meant for; this was the sort of work that she would have spent all day looking forward to, if she had ever been in the habit of looking forward to things. Now it was all she had in the world.

Perhaps some of that showed on her face, because Molly took her hand. "Everything all right, miss?" Her fingers were warm and her touch gentle, and Alice didn't know what to do with either warmth or gentleness. Alice didn't want to look at her eyes to find out whether they shared those qualities. It was taking all her effort to hold on to her knowledge of who she was and what she was made for. The one thing she knew was that a minute too long in Molly Wilkins's company would send her careening far, far out of her place.

"Look at your hands," Molly cooed, kneeling at Miss Stapleton's feet. "Your calluses are nearly gone." She was trying to make conversation, that was all; she just thought it might be nicer for both of them to have a bit of a chat instead of sitting stone-faced in the sewing room hour after hour. After all, Miss Stapleton could have been downstairs in the drawing room where she belonged. But instead she was here, nearly every day, watching.

Molly was used to being watched—by suspicious gentle-folk who knew a thief when they saw one, or by gentlemen with an eye for mischief—but never like this. Sometimes she thought she could actually feel Miss Stapleton's gaze on her flesh, but whenever she glanced over, the lady's eyes were bent down over her work.

She ventured to run her finger along the inside of Miss Stapleton's wrist. When Miss Stapleton first came to Mrs. Wraxhall's house, her hands had been as raw as a washer-woman's. Those hands had scrubbed and polished as much as Molly's own hands, but the poor girl wasn't a farthing the richer for it, and that was a sin and a shame. Molly had spent many an hour wondering what good it was for Miss Stapleton to call herself a lady, when as far as Molly could tell, all it meant was that she was unfit to work for wages but without enough coin to buy so much as a shift.

But Molly knew Miss Stapleton hadn't ever really been a proper lady, not like the ladies Molly had served. Miss Stapleton's dingy gray frocks, all mended and trimmed dozens of times in a way that screamed poverty, had been a good deal shabbier than Molly's own clothes. Mrs. Wraxhall had instructed Molly to ensure that Miss Stapleton's clothing was ruined in the wash. The replacement wardrobe Mrs. Wraxhall insisted on purchasing was much finer, but still boring beyond all reckoning. Never had Molly seen such a proliferation of gray. It was as if Miss Stapleton had her own personal fog that followed her about.

"Have you been using the salve the housekeeper gave you?" she asked.

Miss Stapleton snatched her hand away, so that must have been the wrong thing to say. Chin tilted up, lips pressed tight, dusty blue eyes flashing, she looked at Molly like she had never seen anything so unseemly in her life.

She knows. Molly jumped to her feet and had carefully folded another stack of chemises before remembering that there wasn't anything to know. There wasn't anything to find out, and wasn't that a strange feeling? Molly had been on the straight and narrow for a while now: no bits and bobs of her ladyship's toilette conveniently going missing, no carrying on with the coachman. Only honest work.

Molly had gone into service to get her foot into the door of one of those big Mayfair houses where they just left silver and ivory lying about, where there were gentlemen who might give her a bracelet or a gold coin for her troubles between the sheets instead of the pittance she'd earn in the rookery for the same work. But she had soon realized that compared to the constant threat of Newgate or starvation, life even as a scullery maid was a blessed relief. She stole less and less and worked more and more. Here she was, well-fed and clean, with a position of respect in the household, and enough money to take care of Katie.

That's what she ought to be thinking of now. Not Miss Stapleton's hands, or her eyes, or the mystery of why she sat in the corner of the sewing room like an especially prim shadow. But that was Molly's problem and always had been. She was no good at doing what she ought to. She could almost hear the voices of every housekeeper and butler she had worked under, a couple coppers, and maybe even her ma, if she could remember that far back, all telling her she was no better than a jumped-up gutter snipe, and would come to no good. Well, she couldn't afford to bollocks it up this time. She had more than just herself to think of. And she knew that somehow Alice Stapleton was going to be the ruin of everything she had worked for.

Alice couldn't seem to pry her fingers loose from the parcel. She had tied it up so carefully, with an extra layer of brown paper and double-knotted twine, her sister's name and direction written carefully on the outside as well as on the sheaf of papers within. She had pressed each handkerchief between a sheet of tissue, as she had seen Molly do to Mrs. Wraxhall's delicate gowns.

"Excuse me, Mrs. Wraxhall?"

Alice's benefactress leapt to a start, nearly knocking over her inkwell. "Gracious, Alice! You mustn't go about creeping up on people like that!"

After a lifetime of tiptoeing around her father, shushing her sisters and brothers, calming the beleaguered servants, and overall making herself as invisible as a person could be, Alice was as stealthy as any cat burglar. "I'm so sorry," she said, tittering nervously. "You'll have to tie a bell around my neck, like a cat."

Mrs. Wraxhall put down her pen and regarded Alice's person as if contemplating where a bell could be attached.

"Not a bell, perhaps, but a string of pearls would not be at all amiss . . ." she murmured.

The lady had enough money to deck all the spinsters of Mayfair in ropes of pearls if she so chose, and didn't seem to grasp that her companion was not a doll to be outfitted and adorned at another person's whim. Her father had been a merchant of some sort, and—according to the housekeeper's gossip, which Alice ought to have ignored—had all but purchased his daughter an aristocratic husband. The husband, however, was nowhere to be seen. His bedroom door remained locked, and the only signs that he had ever lived in the house were an unused ashtray that rested near the fire in the drawing room, and a cushion that had evidently been used by his dog. Sometimes Alice caught Mrs. Wraxhall looking wistfully at one or the other of these objects, but the sadness always passed quickly from her face, and she reverted to her usual good cheer.

Alice decided to interrupt before Mrs. Wraxhall actually went so far as to send for her jewel box. "I was wondering if you might have one of your servants, the coachman perhaps, bring this to my sister while you're in Norfolk." She held out the parcel. "If it wouldn't be too much trouble, I mean."

"Why on earth wouldn't you bring it yourself?"

"I have no means to bring it." Sometimes Mrs. Wraxhall needed to be reminded of the facts of life for those not born to wealth and status. Alice had no money to hire a private post chaise and nip over to the vicarage several counties away.

"While we're at Eastgate Hall, you'll use my carriage,"

Mrs. Wraxhall said, in the manner of one explaining the alphabet to a child who ought to have learnt it already.

"No, no," Alice protested, realization dawning. "I'm not going to Eastgate Hall." As if being here in a fine house in London weren't bizarre enough. To start traveling to house parties? Impossible.

"Of course you are. You're my companion. I require your company." She said this with a smile, as if telling Alice of a special treat. "It's not so close to your father's parish that you need to worry about anyone having heard of your . . ." She let her voice trail off.

Alice hadn't even thought of that. Eastgate Hall was perhaps an hour's ride from the village where she had grown up, but she had so seldom ventured farther than the nearest market town, that Eastgate might as well have been as unreachable as Paris or the moon.

"No, I'm not worried about gossip following me to Eastgate Hall." She tried a different line of argument. "The house party will be filled with people who are clever and amusing. You won't need me in the least. I could stay in London and . . ." She desperately rummaged around her brain, trying to think of some excuse to remain, some service she could perform that would warrant her staying in town, but that was the crux of the problem: she had no purpose, either in town or country or anywhere else on earth. She had nothing to do, and no one to do it for.

Mrs. Wraxhall cocked her head. A lock of her carefully curled brown hair had escaped her cap. "Have you no wish to be among clever and amusing people, Alice?"

"I . . . but . . ." Alice sputtered. She would, in fact, rather be burnt at the stake than spend a fortnight at a strange house among people who had in common a wealth and education that she did not share. Every conversation would be like embroidering a flower she had never seen, only heard of second- or third-hand. "I'll oblige you in any way you wish, of course."

Mrs. Wraxhall sighed. "Perhaps you'll meet ladies and gentlemen who will properly appreciate your worth."

No doubt this was meant as a compliment, but Alice knew her worth. She knew it down to the tuppence. She knew that despite her sleepless nights and tireless work, she wasn't worth so much that she couldn't be cast aside with scarcely a backward glance.

Or perhaps Mrs. Wraxhall thought that among the guests, there would be a gentleman—a semi-impoverished curate or a gentleman farmer of the middling sort—who might find it cheaper to take a wife than to hire servants. That would be familiar enough ground. A part of her wanted to jump at the chance to return to a life she understood.

"I doubt my sister will receive me anyway," Alice said in a rare moment of self-pity. "So it doesn't signify." She turned the package over and over, so gingerly, so carefully, when really she could have tossed it into the fireplace for all it mattered. "My letters are always returned unopened."

It had been months since Alice's father had cast her out. Months of silence, months of shame. If it hadn't been for the happenstance of Mrs. Wraxhall—who had her own reasons for seeking to thwart the wishes of imperious men—being near to hand when Alice's misfortune had occurred, Alice would have been without a roof over her head or bread on her plate. As it was, she was lucky. All she had lost was her family, none of whom evidently gave a fig for her. And, of course, she had lost her purpose

"I had heard as much." Mrs. Wraxhall's mouth was a tight line. "But I thought that perhaps if you brought them in person . . ."

"I can hardly act surprised," Alice said, even though a part of her indeed was surprised whenever one of her letters was returned. "Disowning would be rather meaningless if we kept up a correspondence."

"Idiots," Mrs. Wraxhall said under her breath. "Fools."

The paper wrapping the parcel crinkled under Alice's fingers as she clenched her hand. She must have been deluded to think that these silly fripperies could possibly get through to her family when years of Alice's honest work hadn't mattered in the least. She would toss the entire parcel directly into the fire and be rid of it.

"What rankles the most," Mrs. Wraxhall went on, "is that he'll never meet with justice in this world, and I have sadly little faith in justice being meted out in the next."

Alice was momentarily taken aback. Justice was in the same category as diamonds and gold—utterly unavailable to her, and therefore not worth thinking about. She was rather surprised that Mrs. Wraxhall still believed in it. But then again, people clung to stupid ideas long past the point of reason. She glanced at the parcel in her hands. Hope was one of them.

"**O**i!" Molly grabbed Miss Stapleton's wrist and tugged it away from the fire. "Stop that!"

"I beg your pardon!" the lady said, all offended-like, as if Molly were a pickpocket. Her cheeks were red and her eyes blazing bright, and this was the most color Molly had yet seen in her face.

"Won't," Molly said. "Not till that parcel is well away from the fire."

"Have it your way." The lady dropped the little bundle into Molly's hand. "Do what you please with it."

Molly narrowed her eyes. "Really? These the handkerchiefs?" Miss Stapleton nodded. "You spent a couple months squinting over them, and now they're kindling?"

"I don't care what they are." She was in a fine state, was Miss Stapleton.

Molly raised an eyebrow. "Then you don't mind if I sell them?" It said no good things about Molly's character that when confronted with a person on the brink of a towering rage, she had to go the distance and topple them right off the edge.

Molly hadn't expected a loud trill of laughter, though. "Please yourself." Oh, and that little sniff of indignation the lady gave was something special. "I doubt you'd get a shilling for the lot."

"Oh, you're wrong there." Molly knew what a brand-new,

prettily embroidered handkerchief would fetch, because she had stolen and pawned her fair share. A matching set? Now, that would bring a tidy sum to tuck away for Katie. "Maybe a guinea?" she mused aloud.

Well, that got the lady's interest. "A guinea," she repeated.

"Give or take."

Miss Stapleton was silent a moment, her lips slightly parted as if deep in thought. "No," she finally said. "I can't take money for handwork."

"Bugger," Molly answered, not pointing out that she hadn't offered the lady a share of the take.

"I beg your pardon." Miss Stapleton drew herself up, quite affronted.

"Bugger," Molly repeated, annunciating carefully. "Bugger not taking money for your work. You haven't a pot to piss in."

Miss Stapleton's eyes widened. "This is very crass."

"Yeah, it is." Ordinarily Molly observed all the dull proprieties with the gentry, but this lady needed to get her head on straight. "So is starving to death."

"I'm not about to starve," Miss Stapleton protested.

Molly ignored that, because they both knew that the only reason the lady had food in her belly was Mrs. Wraxhall's delight in taking the piss out of that red-faced vicar. Instead, she began to carefully unwrap the parcel, taking out the handkerchiefs one by one.

She let out a low whistle when she saw them spread out before her, snowy linen embellished with a riot of colors. There were a dozen in total, each one of them bearing every color of the rainbow.

"I dare say they're very vulgar," Miss Stapleton said. "It's just as well my sister will never see them."

Molly was about to say that Miss Stapleton's entire family could go straight to hell, where handkerchiefs would be the least of their worries, but something on one of the handkerchiefs caught her eye. "Oh, bless me. Look at that little fellow." An elfin creature peeped out from behind a row of delicately embroidered hollyhocks. She examined another handkerchief and found a tiny fairy, no bigger than the nail on her smallest finger, sleeping inside a daffodil.

And to think, all this for blowing your nose. "My little—" Molly stopped. She had nearly finished that sentence in a way that would have required a good deal of explanation. "They're pretty," she said instead. "Your needlework is very fine."

Miss Stapleton made a noise that from a regular person would be a snort but for which the upper classes likely had some other name. "I certainly have enough practice. But the pictures are only to go with the stories." She gestured to the folded stack of papers that still sat in the remnants of the parcel wrapping.

Molly retrieved the papers and saw they were filled, front and back, with a thin, spidery hand. "Stories?"

"I used to tell fairy stories to my nieces. And since I can't see them anymore, I thought to write them down for my sister to read aloud."

Can't see them, not *don't* see them. Molly knew enough of the events surrounding Miss Stapleton's banishment to make a guess. "I know your father tossed you out. Your sister was in on it too?"

The lady swallowed, as if deciding whether Molly was worth a confidence. "My sister doesn't care to disoblige our father. None of my siblings do."

"Spineless," Molly spat.

The lady's eyes went wide and something flickered across her face. Gratitude? Disgust? Whatever it was, it didn't last long, because she tossed her head and swept from the room as grandly as a lady could in a dreary gray frock.

Chapter Two

The lady's maid sneaked out whenever Mrs. Wraxhall dined away from home, Alice was certain of it. Last night Alice had gone into Mrs. Wraxhall's boudoir in search of a headache powder, and the door to the adjoining maid's bedroom had been open, the room clearly empty. Nor had the woman been downstairs. The hour was too late for her to conceivably be running an errand for Mrs. Wraxhall, and the only question in Alice's mind was whether the maid was carrying on with a man or engaged in something even more nefarious.

Tonight, Mrs. Wraxhall was dining out again, and Alice had pleaded to be excused on the grounds that her headache had returned. She sat in the back parlor, by a window that overlooked the mews. Her hands felt empty, pointless, when holding neither pen nor needle, but she could hardly bring herself to begin another doomed handkerchief or another story that would never be read. She leaned back in the too-soft chair and adjusted the draperies so she could see the precise place where the kitchen door opened below.

It didn't take long before Molly appeared. Even covered head to toe in a black cloak, she was unmistakable, and Alice could make out the sway of her hips and slight swagger of her walk. Alice leapt up and flew down the back stairs on silent feet. She already had on her warmest pelisse, a measure that had earlier felt like wise planning and now smelled like premeditation. Never mind that. She slipped past the bustling kitchen servants and made for the mews.

Molly cut through alleys and passageways with the brisk efficiency of a woman who had traveled this route many times before, taking corners diagonally and not sparing a glance for her surroundings. This shadowy web of streets was Molly's natural habitat.

Alice, her thoughts divided between keeping Molly in sight and the necessity of not tripping over the hem of her gown, scarcely noticed where they were heading until she realized she was in an entirely unfamiliar part of London. During her few months in town, Alice had only traveled on foot the distance from Mrs. Wraxhall's front door to the carriage and back again; she had certainly never ventured this far east. At least—she checked over her shoulder, towards where the sun appeared to be setting behind buildings she had never seen before—she was fairly certain this was east.

Finally, after Alice's ankle boots started to pinch her toes and her fingers had gone numb in her useless kidskin gloves,

Molly came to a stop in front of a low brick building. Alice watched as the lady's maid rapped on the door before stepping wordlessly inside. So, she had been expected by her . . . paramour, or whatever a man was supposed to be called in these situations.

Whatever the case, this was a decidedly inauspicious place for an assignation. It wasn't precisely a bad neighborhood, but down at the heels and worn around the edges. In the great divide between gentry and commoner, this row of houses was planted a few crucial inches on the side of the common. Alice, having spent her life helping her family cling to their station a few inches over on the opposite side of the divide, knew the signs of not-quite-gentility all too well: a couple of chickens had strayed out into the street, a few bits of forgotten washing hung in the gap between two houses, an ownerless dog wandered hungrily about the pavements.

It was not the place Alice would have chosen for a romantic interlude, if she were in the business of having interludes of any variety—which, of course, she was not.

Now, though, she had a problem greater than Molly's bad behavior. She had set out on this harebrained mission without any definite plan, with the result that she was standing, conspicuous and cold, in front of a strange building in an unfamiliar quarter, with the sun rapidly setting, and no idea how to get back to Mrs. Wraxhall's house.

The dog began eying her suspiciously.

She would need to wait until Molly reappeared, and then follow her home. Molly couldn't stay inside indefinitely—

surely she meant to return well before Mrs. Wraxhall. But it was not unheard of for Mrs. Wraxhall to stay out well past midnight.

Alice's warmest pelisse did not feel warm at all. She missed the heavy wool cloak that Mrs. Wraxhall had declared unfit for London. This was the first time she had been cold since leaving the vicarage. It was funny, how one got out of the practice of being uncomfortable. The cold greeted Alice like an old friend.

Was Molly warm, in her lover's embrace? Alice really didn't want to think about that; honestly, she went out of her way never to imagine Molly other than clothed and upright, but now she had a vision of curving hips and swaying breasts, a throaty laugh, a crooked smile.

"You lost, miss?" The voice came from far too near Alice's shoulder. She spun around to see a strange man in a soft cap.

"N-no," she stuttered.

Even in the darkness, Alice could see the skepticism on the stranger's face. "You look lost. Let me hail a hackney?"

Alice drew herself up. "That won't be necessary."

The man reached out to take her elbow—maybe only to usher her towards safety, towards a hackney.

But it didn't matter. Alice screamed.

Molly was nearly at the end of Katie's bedtime story when she heard a sound like a cat being murdered.

"Oh for God's sake," she muttered, putting aside the page she had been reading. She rose to her feet, shifting the now-wide-awake Katie to her hip. This was Holborn—well, almost Holborn—not Seven Dials. One didn't expect murder to happen in the middle of the street. That was why Molly paid so dearly to keep Katie here—it was safe and clean, certainly safer and cleaner than the rookery where Molly had grown up.

She pulled the curtain back enough to get a look at the street. It was dark, but in the moonlight she saw a flash of pale blond hair beneath a bonnet. Squinting, she could make out a dove-gray pelisse trimmed with slate-gray braid.

She knew that hair, had spent many a misbegotten moment wondering if it were as silky as it looked, had thought about bribing the housemaid who attended Miss Stapleton to feign illness so Molly could brush out that hair herself. She knew that pelisse too, because she had noticed that a bit of the trim had come down, and had tacked it up with her own hands. For all the time the lady spent with a needle in hand, she never seemed to notice when her own things needed tending to.

"Katie, sit with Mrs. Fitz for a minute, will you?"

The woman automatically held out her hands to receive the child. She loved Katie and did a fine job taking care of her, but Molly felt a surge of resentment at having to let go of her daughter one minute sooner than she had planned. God knew she already got precious little time with the girl. And all for the purpose of rescuing busybody ladies who stuck their noses where they didn't belong.

Molly ran down the stairs and threw open the door. "Johnny, get your hands off her. Have you run mad?"

"I'm not the one who's mad," the landlady's son retorted. "I was offering to get her a hackney and she went daft on me."

Molly cut him a glare. It didn't matter if he was telling the truth. In her experience, lads generally deserved a nasty glare and Molly was willing to do her part.

"You." She turned to Miss Stapleton, who even in the dark was red with embarrassment.

"I—"

"Spare me." As if Molly needed to be told what had brought this lady here. It was nosiness or malice or both. "You ought to be glad Mrs. Wraxhall took you in, because if you were left up to your own devices you'd starve. You haven't the sense God gave a duck." Miss Stapleton's eyes were downcast, her fists balled tightly at her sides, and now Molly felt bad for having spoken harshly. Sighing, Molly said, "Never mind that. Get inside." She threw another menacing look over her shoulder at Johnny, who had his hands raised in helpless protest. "Up the stairs, second door on the right."

It was always a bit of a shock, seeing the right people in the wrong places, and the sight of Miss Stapleton in Mrs. Fitz's flat, two paces away from Katie herself, didn't add up in Molly's mind.

"Mama!" Katie said, as she always did when Molly walked through the door.

"Katie, love," Molly answered, bending to scoop the child into her arms as Mrs. Fitz left the room. "Now you know," she told Miss Stapleton, who had a look of almost comical astonishment on her face. "I suppose you'll try to get me sacked." Molly held Katie closer.

"No," Miss Stapleton said immediately. "It's none of my—"

"That's right, it isn't. Mrs. Wraxhall already knows anyway, so you can spare yourself the trouble."

"I thought . . ." Miss Stapleton shifted from foot to foot, hands clasped before her. "I knew you were sneaking out—"

"Not sneaking," Molly said from behind gritted teeth. She didn't have the patience for this. She had so little time with her daughter as it was, the rare hour in the evening or a half day on Sundays, barely enough for the child to know who she was, and she'd be damned if she was going to waste another minute explaining herself. "I told you, Mrs. Wraxhall already knows."

"I didn't know that, and I only thought to look into the matter for Mrs. Wraxhall in case you were . . ." Her voice trailed off, some genteel delicacy preventing her from saying aloud precisely what she thought Molly had done.

"You thought I was nicking the silver or meeting with a fancy man." There had been a time when Molly had done both of those things, often and with great enthusiasm, and she rather wished she could protest complete innocence. Instead, she raised an eyebrow and glared at her accuser.

"Elf in tree!" Katie tugged a lock of Molly's hair to get her mother's attention. "Elf," she insisted. "Tree." She was almost three and had recently discovered that by saying words, she often got things. "Mama. Elf. Tree."

"She wants me to finish her bedtime story," Molly said. And that was well and good, but Molly had no intention of telling the story with Miss Stapleton hovering by the door. "Sorry, love, but I'll read you the story another time."

"The elf in the tree?" Miss Stapleton murmured almost to herself, her brows drawing together. "Is it a cherry tree?" she asked Katie.

"Cherry! Elf!" Katie agreed, clapping her fat little baby hands.

Molly watched in dismay as Miss Stapleton's eyes searched the room, finally alighting on the stack of papers on the table. "Are those my stories?" she asked, her voice thin and strained.

"Well. You were about to throw them in the fire, so I thought you wouldn't mind." Molly knew she didn't need to feel guilty, but she did anyway. She had enough guilt left over from the past that sometimes it seeped out where it didn't belong. "You might as well sit," she said grudgingly, gesturing to the chair Mrs. Fitz had been sitting in.

When Katie had still been a babe in arms, Molly spent a week's wages on a prettily bound book of children's stories, only to discover that each story culminated in a child being punished and shamed for acts of a naughtiness so mild that Molly wanted to throw the book out the nearest window. She knew theft and violence and the rest of the ways she had kept body and soul together were wrong; she wasn't some kind of heathen. But she couldn't get herself exercised about fictional children stealing muffins when a few streets away there were children who would risk their lives for a chance to steal a loaf of bread. Molly wasn't proud of the stealing and cheating she had done, but she didn't regret it either, because what was a gentleman's watch fob compared to a month of meals in her belly?

When Miss Stapleton said she had written stories for her nieces, Molly expected them to be packed with dull moralizing and heaping with shame. She had thought that maybe they would be a bucket of cold water over whatever embers of warmth she felt for Miss Stapleton. Instead she had found page after page of elves and fairies cavorting about and getting into harmless mischief. There had been no sermonizing, no punishment, only, well, fun. She hadn't thought Miss Stapleton capable of anything even in the neighborhood of fun. Looking at her now—straight-backed, pale-faced, worn out from an evening of high-minded snooping—she seemed about as dry as dust. But now Molly knew she might actually like Miss Stapleton, and she rather wished she didn't.

The child had Molly's honey-brown hair and eyes to match, and clung to her mother's neck as she listened to the tale of the elf in the cherry tree. She was too young to follow the story, and before long the cadence of her mother's voice lulled her to sleep, her little hands unclasping and falling to her sides, her head dropping back against Molly's arm.

Alice's lap felt empty. She had put her nieces to bed like that countless times—stories told in hushed tones, babies held in aching arms. She'd likely never see her nieces again, and even if she managed to worm her way back into her family's good graces, the girls might be half grown by then, well beyond the age for stories and cuddles.

Now she had tears prickling in her eyes, and that would not do at all. She had already embarrassed herself just by coming here. If she started crying, she'd look a proper bedlamite.

A gray-haired woman appeared in the doorway. Molly carefully rose to her feet and passed her the sleeping child, then dug in her pockets for a few coins to slide into the woman's apron pocket. She must spend all her wages keeping her daughter here—the room was clean and quiet, the air was fresh by London standards, and the child was plump and rosy-cheeked.

"You," Molly said to Alice, not meeting her eyes. "Come on."

Outside, night had fallen and the wind was bitterly cold. Alice tried to wrap her pelisse more tightly around herself, but the cold seeped through the layers of wool and silk right to her bones.

"It's less than half an hour if we walk quickly," Molly said, her gaze straight ahead. "You'll live."

"Perhaps we ought to take a hackney?" Walking through a strange part of London in the dark, unaccompanied by a man, seemed a poor idea regardless of the weather. "I have a few shillings."

"Bollocks on shillings," Molly said, striding briskly along the pavements. "Bollocks on hackneys. I always walk, and since you've decided to tail me, you'll walk too."

Alice felt the heat of embarrassment spread through her body, the only warmth in her. "I do apologize—"

"Bollocks on that too."

Alice didn't quite know how to argue with that. She wasn't accustomed to hearing coarse language. For all her father's faults, he had always spoken like a gentleman, although now it occurred to Alice that she might prefer a bit of honest profanity to the alternating miseries of crockery-throwing and sermonizing. Surely she ought to be shocked and insulted to hear herself addressed in such a rude and common manner, but she found that Molly's vulgar words gave her a frisson of excitement. Molly's total lack of deference, her failure to stand on ceremony with a gentlewoman, ought to feel like an insult, but instead made Alice feel warm despite the chill in the air.

"Are you quite certain it's safe?" Alice ventured.

"Lord," Molly said with a huff of laughter. "I'd like to see anybody try and bother us. I've three knives and a reputation for bloodshed."

Good *God*. What did that even *mean*?

"The only real danger is that you might freeze to death," Molly continued. "Do they not have weather in Norfolk or wherever it is you're from?"

Oh, if she only knew how cold it had gotten at the vicarage. "I used to wear wool stockings and flannel petticoats. Sometimes three or four petticoats at a time." And so many shawls that she now felt quite naked without one.

Molly was silent a moment. "And now you don't." There was something in her voice that Alice couldn't quite make out. Something a bit rough.

"Of course not. You know perfectly well what undergarments ladies wear in London. Only a chemise and a couple of thin petticoats. I don't even wear a corset most days. You dress Mrs. Wraxhall several times a day. You know all this."

"Yeah, but I don't think about it." Before Alice could reflect on whether this meant that Molly thought about Alice's underthings, or lack thereof, Molly spoke briskly. "Anyway. Come close. I don't know how either of us would explain it to Mrs. Wraxhall if you caught a chill. Last thing I need is a corpse." She tugged Alice against her, looping her arm through Alice's.

Alice nearly lost her footing at the warmth and softness of the other woman. She almost tripped over her feet and landed in a gutter.

Worse, she nearly pressed closer into Molly's side, trying to feel that softness with her own body.

And then she did it anyway.

Molly smelled like Mrs. Wraxhall's eau de toilette—either she helped herself or some of the perfume had rubbed off her mistress's garments—mixed with the sweet, soapy smell of babies. It was such a normal scent, the sort of thing any woman might smell like. She did not know why she had expected Molly to smell like mystery and intrigue, foreign perfumes and rich musk. Instead she smelled like a person who had a job and a child and a purpose in life, not merely a vague infinity of breasts and hips and crooked grins.

From time to time, Alice found herself looking a little too closely, too warmly, at a woman. At home it had been the curate's sister, then the landlady at the inn. At first, she reassured herself that everyone must have this difficulty: women's bodies were just *good* and one did enjoy looking at good things. One didn't want to ogle, but it was like admiring a particularly well-iced cake, that was all. Perfectly natural. Later, she had to acknowledge that her thoughts about women did not much resemble her thoughts about cake, however well-iced. So she averted her eyes and kept herself busy and tried not to think overmuch about what any of it meant.

With Molly this close she had to think about it.

Molly stopped walking and cleared her throat. Alice frantically scrambled for something to say to explain why she was pressing up against Molly's body like a cat, but tonight she was behaving like a lunatic and couldn't even manage the simplest excuse for her actions. It was as if she hadn't amassed a lifetime of experience in placating and excusing. She settled for the next best thing, which was straightening her back and trying to pull away.

But Molly's arm now wrapped around Alice's waist, tight as a vise.

"You're cold all the way through," Molly said. Then the arm was gone, and Molly was pulling off her own cloak and wrapping it around Alice.

"But you'll get cold," Alice protested.

"I've been colder."

So had Alice, but she was out of practice.

Molly pulled the cloak tight across Alice's chest, but then apparently forgot to remove her arms, because she stood so

close to Alice that their breaths mingled into a single cloud
in freezing air.

Molly hadn't intended to be gallant, and she certainly
wasn't in the habit of sacrificing her comfort for anybody, but
the sight of Miss Stapleton shivering, embarrassed, and obvi-
ously afraid had affected her. Molly wanted to do more than
wrap the lady in a cloak. She wanted to tuck her close, hold
her closer, and think of interesting ways to rub some warmth
back into that rail-thin body.

The girl needed hot soup.

And kissing.

And more. Molly had very clear ideas of what *more*
might consist of, even if it had been a while since she had
put any of those ideas to practical use.

She'd give it good odds that Miss Stapleton was interested in *more* as well, whether she knew it or not. Whether
she'd let herself was another question entirely, one Molly
didn't intend to find out the answer to. Molly had a decent
life working for Mrs. Wraxhall. She wasn't likely to find
another employer who would look the other way when her
maid disappeared to care for an illegitimate daughter, and
she wasn't going to throw away Katie's chance at a decent
future for a quick tumble.

No matter how much she wanted to.

So now Molly was shivering in her black wool frock, and
Miss Stapleton was shivering in her gown, pelisse, and cloak,

and Molly still had her arms wrapped around the lady. Really, they ought to move. This was not the time to be dallying in the shadows, and Miss Stapleton was nobody to dally with either. But Molly liked the feel of her, and judging by the way Miss Stapleton sort of melted against her, she liked it too.

Miss Stapleton pulled back a fraction of an inch, just enough for Molly to get a good look at her. "You won't be able to see her when we're in Norfolk at the house party," the lady whispered.

Thank God for the bit of moonlight shining on the lady's face, or Molly might have thought Miss Stapleton was rubbing Molly's nose in misfortune. But there was no mistaking the bleakness in the other woman's eyes.

"It's happened before, and it's—" She nearly said that it was fine, that it was part of her job, that she didn't mind. But those were all lies. "I miss her something awful." Molly swallowed, fisting the wool of the cloak in her hand and feeling Miss Stapleton sway closer. "And I think she misses me, but sometimes I think she might not. And I don't know if that makes it better or worse."

The lady sucked in a breath and briefly shut her eyes, as if she had stepped on a tack.

Molly remembered what she had heard about Miss Stapleton serving as a glorified governess for her sister's children and housekeeper for her father. At the time, Molly had thought it a shame that the girl hadn't even been paid for her servitude, and then was turned loose into the cold. And that was before she had seen the handkerchiefs meant for tiny hands, read the stories intended for little ears.

"Right," Molly said. "You'll know about how that is, won't you." The lady nodded once, looking grateful not to have to explain herself. "We ought to keep moving if we don't want to freeze."

Molly kept her arm entwined with the lady's the rest of the way home.

CHAPTER THREE

"Please let me unpick that trim," Alice asked for the fifth
time.

"No. It's my work. Get your own post as a lady's maid if
you want to unpick trim so badly."

"But I don't want to embroider any more handkerchiefs"—
she could hardly bring herself to do so, knowing they'd never
be seen by her nieces—"and helpful elves have mended the
spencer I meant to work on." She cast Molly a pointed glance;
the maid didn't look up from her sewing, but Alice thought
she saw a smile. "I'll go quite mad if I have to sit here with
nothing to do."

"Then go downstairs. Mrs. Wraxhall has company.
There will be cake."

Alice did not know what to do in a roomful of people
who were meant for nothing but cake and idleness. She
knew she was supposed to welcome this as her birthright
as the daughter of a gentleman, but she'd much rather be
put to use scouring pans in the kitchen. No, if Alice went

downstairs, she would sit in the hard-backed chair farthest from the fire. She would be silent and still, hoping nobody took any notice of her. This didn't seem like a very good reason to go downstairs, and it was occurring to Alice that she didn't have to do anything she didn't want to do. This was not an entirely welcome realization after a lifetime during which her wants hadn't mattered in the slightest. The laundry had needed hanging, the soup needed stirring, the baby needed rocking; Alice had done her duty, and that was that. The absence of duty left her with nothing other than want as her guiding principle, and the thought made her feel adrift.

"There will be cake," Molly repeated in a wheedling, singsong tone.

Alice made a dismissive noise. "Bollocks on cake," she said, borrowing Molly's phrase.

Molly looked up in mock affront. "Never say that about cake."

Alice giggled, actually giggled. She couldn't remember the last time she'd done that.

"Well, suit yourself," Molly said, tossing Alice a gown that needed some beads resewn before it could be worn again. "If you want to do my job, I shan't stop you."

They sewed together for the rest of the afternoon, and sometimes when Alice looked across the room, Molly gave her a sly little sideways smile. The first time, Alice nearly dropped her work because that smile somehow put her in mind of secret nighttime thoughts she was trying not to reflect overmuch on. The second time, she returned a smile of her own—not a crooked nighttime-thought kind of smile, but a smile that was meant for Molly. It was the only kind of smile Alice had, and it would have to do.

The third time, Molly moved so they were sitting beside one another on the same settee.

When the dinner hour drew near, Molly rose to her feet and stretched. "A letter came from the Continent today, so that means Mrs. Wraxhall will take her supper on a tray in bed. I'd better see if she needs a warming pan."

"A letter from the Continent?"

"That's where Mr. Wraxhall is."

"Is he on a diplomatic mission?"

"Oh lord no. He's drying out in some spa town."

"Drying—what on earth are you talking about?" Alice had an image of Mr. Wraxhall, son of a baronet, husband of an heiress, hanging out laundry somewhere in Belgium.

"He drank. A lot. He's gone to the Continent so he can get in the habit of not doing that anymore. Not sure why he couldn't dry out just as well in London, but people who have money like to find ways to spend it, I guess."

Alice wasn't sure about that. She could see how breaking a habit might be easier if one wasn't surrounded by familiar temptations. She had often thought that if only she were able to stop the wine merchant from extending credit to her father, a good deal of their household's troubles could have been avoided. "Why didn't Mrs. Wraxhall go with him?"

"Beats me. I think he was embarrassed by some trouble he caused. The poor lady was in a wretched state last summer." Before Alice could ask about what this trouble was, Molly continued speaking. "If you ask me, she doesn't think he'll come back, which is why she gets herself worked up when a letter comes from him. Oh! Before I forget," she said, reaching her hand into her pocket. "This is for you." In her palm was a golden guinea, two crowns, and several shillings.

"I beg your pardon?"

"For the handkerchiefs. I sold them."

"You sold them?"

"You said I could," Molly protested, sounding offended.

"No, I quite appreciate it. Thank you. I just never thought to get so much money for them." She reached towards Molly's outstretched hand but didn't touch the coins. It seemed impossible that she had money of her own. Money she had earned, not begged off her father, not been given as charity by Mrs. Wraxhall.

Molly took hold of her wrist and dumped the coins into Alice's palm, where they landed with an impossibly bright clinking. Then Molly clasped Alice's hand, the coins in between their palms, and said, "You deserve it," before leaving Alice alone.

Even when things had gone very poorly at the vicarage—even the sort of "poorly" that involved crockery being thrown across the room and the housemaid cowering in the larder—Alice never got angry. There was no point to it. Her father had been angry enough for the two of them, and meeting his anger with some of her own would only have earned her the same treatment as the crockery. She had gotten into the habit of brushing off any inconvenient emotion like she might brush dust off the chimneypiece, and simply getting down to the business of setting things right.

Now that she lived a life of outrageous idleness, in a house with functioning chimneys and meals that appeared on the table as if by magic, she found herself furious over the least things.

When they arrived at Eastgate Hall and she learned that she was to share a room with Molly, she nearly cried with helpless annoyance. As if she hadn't shared a bedroom nearly every night of her life before coming to Mrs. Wraxhall's house. As if she didn't still reach out in the night to comfort a sibling or niece who wasn't there.

"Her ladyship doesn't want either of us sleeping next door to her bedchamber," Molly said as she unpacked the perfumes and salves and combs and ribbons that were required in her mistress's toilette. They were in the dressing room that adjoined Mrs. Wraxhall's bedchamber; this was where Molly would have made a bed for herself if Mrs. Wraxhall hadn't decreed otherwise at the last minute, when it was too late for any arrangement to be made besides the lady's maid and the companion sharing quarters. "If you ask me," Molly said, arranging a pair of ivory hair combs on the dressing table, "she has a fellow."

"Nobody did ask you," Alice snapped. Molly turned, her mouth an O, her eyebrows nearly at her hairline. She didn't look insulted, so much as impressed, as if she hadn't thought Alice had it in her to snap at anyone. Alice had hardly thought so herself.

"That was unkind of me," she said, falling back on the old habit of contrition. "I apologize." Besides, who was she to begrudge Mrs. Wraxhall some comfort and companionship? Her husband had been gone for several months and might never return. "I suppose that's what people do at these parties." Alice was conscious that any decent woman would come up with some suitable comment about dens of iniquity or some such. Her father certainly would have expected it of her.

Perhaps for that reason alone, Alice kept silent. What did it matter to her whether Mrs. Wraxhall carried on with every gentleman in East Anglia? She was a kind, charitable woman—witness Alice's continued existence—and if fornication was what she required to sustain that level of good humor and generosity, then so be it.

"Some do," Molly answered, as if Alice's question had been anything other than rhetorical. "Others just gossip and gamble and ride horses, pretty much like they do every other day of the year. What'll you do?"

Was she asking whether Alice intended to have an affair? "Not lift my skirts for some man," she said before she could consider the wisdom of such a response. "No doubt there are dowagers in attendance who require their yarn to be balled up and children who need their dollies mended. Those tasks seem much less tedious to me than entertaining gentlemen."

Molly let out a peal of laughter. "Oh Christ. You and me both. More trouble than they're worth, the lot of them."

Maybe the sound of Molly's laughter was as intoxicating as Mrs. Wraxhall's bubbly wine, because Alice found herself asking the worst possible question. "You must have thought otherwise at some point. With Katie's father, I mean."

Molly went still, holding a pincushion in midair, and too late Alice realized that Katie's father might have been the kind of brute who took what he wanted without a thought to spare for anyone else. Alice had learned that lesson well.

"He promised me a silver locket," Molly said, with a look that dared Alice to judge her.

"Did he deliver?"

"No. I blackmailed him, though."

"Good," Alice said, with more venom than she thought she possessed.

"Miss Stapleton," Molly said, shaking her head in feigned admonishment.

Alice made a dismissive sound. "Did he give you enough so you can put a bit aside for Katie when she's older? So she can . . ." Alice didn't know what the children of servants and blackmailed gentlemen did when they came of age. "Learn a trade?" Alice's own money had been put aside for her marriage, but as she had never married, her father had simply kept it. And now she'd never see it.

"Her money's safe and I don't need to touch it. My wages are enough to keep her at Mrs. Fitz's and maybe send her to school in a few years."

Alice felt a surge of—it couldn't possibly be affection, but something near enough to it—towards this woman who had thought to properly set money aside for her daughter. "How lucky your daughter is to have a parent who looks out for her."

Molly pursed her lips. "Not a lot of people would call the bastard daughter of a lightskirt lucky."

Alice wanted to deny it, but Molly was right. "Many people would think the daughter of a reasonably prosperous clergyman was very lucky indeed. But I expect your Katie will never have a parent who harms her." She spoke the words lightly, carefully, but Molly looked at her sharply all the same.

"I wonder what that's like," Molly said.

Alice was overwhelmed by this sudden sense of common feeling with a woman whose life had been so different from her own, but who had wound up in roughly the same place. Grasping for something more familiar, she noticed that one of Mrs. Wraxhall's chemises had a hem that had come untacked. "If we're to share a room, you might as well let me share some of the mending," she said, reaching for the garment.

Quick as a bolt, Molly reached out and grabbed Alice's hand, stopping her from taking the chemise. Alice's first instinct was to snatch her hand back, but when Molly didn't let go, instead she let herself enjoy the touch. It was mere friendliness, she told herself. It was all right to enjoy the warmth and the gentleness, and Molly wouldn't have touched her if she didn't want to. So she put her other hand over Molly's, letting her fingers slip between the other woman's. She kept her gaze there, at their interlocked fingers, not daring to look up at Molly's face. The silence between them stretched out, neither of them moving. They were holding hands, and the only reason they were doing it was that they both wanted to. They wanted to touch one another. There was no escaping from that basic fact: Alice wanted, and was wanted in return.

Finally, she cleared her throat. "I'd like to help. I hate being idle." That was the truth, and it felt strange to admit it—as if she were confessing to something more improper than a fondness for work. "And you know my stitchwork is good."

Molly snorted. "It's wasted on a hem."

"But that's what I like to do. Decent, simple work. I don't need to adorn things. I like to do the kind of work that matters to people." She missed it terribly. Her fingers itched to be useful. "The kind that helps the people I'm fond of."

Molly regarded her for a moment, then tugged Alice's hand so she had to come closer or let go. Alice stepped forward, and now their boots were almost touching, their hands clasped together. She stood perfectly still, staring fixedly at Molly's shoulder.

"And you're fond of Mrs. Wraxhall?" Alice didn't need to look to know that Molly had that sly, crooked smile playing across her lips.

Alice was indeed very fond of Mrs. Wraxhall, so she nodded.

"And of me, too, aren't you?"

Alice closed her eyes to avoid the temptation of looking at Molly's mouth. She nodded again.

"Good," Molly said, and it was little more than a breath. Alice could nearly feel it on her cheek.

Molly stepped back, and Alice let go of her hand. But as Alice sat in the chair by the window, avoiding looking at the too-familiar Norfolk countryside, her hands deftly restitching the fallen hem, she thought she could feel the echoes of that warm touch on her skin for the rest of the afternoon.

"I think," Molly said, much later, "it's high time I called you Alice."

Molly woke at dawn, startled to find a slender, pale arm draped across her chest. She wouldn't have figured Miss Stapleton—Alice—for a cuddler.

She rolled to face her bedmate, enjoying the closeness. She didn't get much of that these days. It was time to get out of bed, time to make sure Mrs. Wraxhall's gowns bore no creases, that her tea had the correct amount of sugar, that the stableman was prepared to saddle her horse at the appointed hour. Through the chimneys, she could hear the faint clatter of the household getting down to the business of the day. If she didn't get started herself, she'd pay the price the rest of the morning.

But still she stayed in bed, watching the rise and fall of Alice's chest and the way her breath rustled a single lock of moonshine hair. Only when Alice stirred did Molly make a great show of yawning and stretching, acting like she had just awoken.

"Oh!" Alice said, snatching her arm away from Molly. "I'm sorry!"

"About what?" Molly said sleepily, as if she hadn't noticed the arm, as if she couldn't still feel the warmth from where Alice had touched her. She got out of bed and stretched again, and this time she saw Alice watching her out of the corner of her eye. From a man, it would be a leer. Maybe from Alice it was a leer, too. Molly rather suspected it was, for all Alice was a fine lady.

Molly took her time at the washstand, conscious of Alice's gaze on her. Finally she threw a look over her shoulder, catching Alice in the act.

"I'm sorry," Alice said, pink guilt splashed across her face. Damn it if Molly weren't well and truly tired of all this sorriness. Bollocks on apologies. Bollocks on guilt.

"Nah," Molly said, raising her arms over her head in a way she knew did something special to her bosom. Alice's eyes widened in response. "Nothing to be sorry for. You can look all you like."

"Oh heavens," Alice squeaked, diving under the quilt.

"It's only natural," Molly argued, feeling wicked and righteous all at once.

"No," Alice said, her voice muffled by the bedclothes, "it's just that I haven't any of my own, not really. Not like you do."

Oh no. That would not do at all. Such a bad excuse was even worse than the pink, embarrassed apologies. Molly crawled across the bed towards the lump under the covers that was Alice. "That's not why you look at them, though."

"I don't know what you could possibly mean." Alice sounded as haughty as was possible from under a quilt.

"Just what I said." Molly poked what she guessed was Alice's backside. "You haven't any bollocks, but John the footman has a pair of them. I don't see you trying to get an eyeful of that, though."

"An eyeful of bollocks, indeed." Alice's indignant face popped out from under the covers. "I have no interest in John the footman's bollocks, nor anybody else's."

"That's right, you don't," Molly said cheerfully. "You're more interested in bosoms."

"That's not what I said!" The pink of embarrassment was replaced with a pink that meant something else entirely, unless Molly was very much mistaken.

"It's all right, though," Molly said, all reassurance. "I like to look at yours too."

Alice gasped and tightened her fingers on the quilt, as if to pull it up to her chin. But she didn't. "I don't have anything to look at—"

"Sure you do." Molly rested her hand on the edge of the quilt and raised an eyebrow. She wasn't going to do this without the go-ahead. "I bet they're sweet." Alice obligingly dropped her hands away, and Molly drew the quilt down. Through the thin linen of Alice's shift, Molly could see the outline of Alice's breasts, her nipples tightening before Molly's eyes. Molly licked her lips. She wanted to bend her head and take one in her mouth. Alice's lips were slightly parted and her expression a bit dazed. She liked this, being looked at, being wanted and a bit exposed. God help her, Molly could think of a dozen different ways to use that bit of information, but there wasn't time for anything now, not if she wanted to keep her job. And Molly needed this job. She shouldn't even have done this much. She ought to already be downstairs, not lazing about in the bedroom, seducing vicars' daughters.

Gently, Molly raised the edge of the coverlet to just beneath Alice's chin. Then she threw her dress over her head, knotted her hair plainly in the back, stepped into her boots, and left the room before Alice could reappear.

Chapter Four

Much to Alice's relief, there was plenty of work to be done at a house party. Despite Mrs. Wraxhall spending the morning out riding, Alice kept herself busy by managing the tricky bits of embroidery for a lady who was too busy catching up on gossip with her friends to be bothered with the fussier aspects of needlework. That suited Alice quite well, as it gave her an excuse to be silent without looking awkward. She felt that she blended in most unobjectionably, almost as if she were a standard-issue lady, rather than a shabby lady's companion who was thinking of doing unspeakable acts with a servant.

She snipped a length of emerald-green thread and attended to the gossip.

"I heard he wasn't coming this year. Something about having to dance attendance on a wealthy aunt," said the lady whose cushion Alice was doctoring.

"Then why would the housemaids be readying a bed-chamber for him this very morning?" asked her interlocutor with a smile that spelled victory.

"Well! That changes things."

"I should say it does. It changes what I'll be wearing at dinner, for one."

They tittered. "He's handsome, but he's dangling after a rich wife."

"What do I care what kind of wife he wants? Not a fig, that's what. My plans for Horace Tenpenny have nothing to do with marriage."

At the sound of that name, Alice sucked in a breath of air. She had hoped never to hear it again, but of course couldn't be so lucky, not with Mr. Tenpenny traveling in circles not so different from Mrs. Wraxhall's own. And now he was to be here, in this house, at the dinner table with her? She clutched the embroidery in her hand, and then gasped when she realized she had pricked herself on the needle. Before she could collect herself, a bead of bright red blood had formed on her fingertip and dropped onto the cushion. "Oh no!" she cried. "I've quite ruined your work!"

"Oh, bother my work," said the lady. "You've done most of it yourself anyway. Stevens, ring for a plaster for Miss Stapleton, will you?" As if to underscore her point, she threw the embroidery, hoop and all, into the fire. Alice yelped anew, because surely some of the piece could have been salvaged, some corner with which to make a pincushion or a coin purse. That was, somehow, a more potent reminder of Alice's unbelonging than even the news that the odious Mr. Tenpenny would be arriving.

Pleading the necessity of tending to her wound, which had already stopped bleeding and would soon be nothing more than the ghost of a pinprick, Alice went upstairs as quickly as was compatible with dignity. She would feign illness and stay in her bed the remainder of the house party. That was the only way. Facing Mr. Tenpenny was out of the question.

But staying in bed meant more time around Molly. Molly, who *knew*. Molly, who had caught her looking, which was bad enough. What was worse was that Molly hadn't seemed to mind. Alice knew how to handle outrage—she could have apologized, she could have tried to disappear in a cloud of polite self-recrimination. But Molly had only responded with blithe acceptance and then gone on to do some looking of her own.

Perhaps she could borrow enough from Mrs. Wraxhall to take the stagecoach back to London. But the house in Grosvenor Square was closed up for the next month while Mrs. Wraxhall attended a succession of house parties. There was nowhere for Alice to go.

She flung open her bedroom door and shut it quickly behind her, as if she were being chased by a pack of wolves.

"Lord help me," Molly exclaimed, leaping up from the table where she was sewing silk flowers to a pair of dancing slippers. "Are you all right?" Petals were scattered at her feet.

"Yes, quite." Alice was struggling to catch her breath, and the words came out as more air than sound. "I'm fine."

"Well, that's a lie. What happened?"

Alice contemplated making an excuse, but then figured she had nothing to lose. After this morning, was this sordid tale likely to make a difference? "It's only that I didn't realize that Mr. Tenpenny was going to be here."

"Oh?"

"I can't meet him again." Alice wrung her hands. It was one thing to decide to tell the story; it was another thing entirely to find the words. She finally settled on, "He's the reason I was sent from home."

Molly's eyes opened wide in confusion, before narrowing to slits. "You . . . you and this Tenpenny fellow?"

"No!" Alice lay on the bed, staring at the ceiling. The words might be easier to say if she didn't have to watch Molly's reaction. "He . . . did something untoward, and I was blamed."

"He touched you?" Alice could hear the fury in Molly's voice. The last time she had told this mortifying tale, there had been fury in her father's voice, but that time the anger had been directed towards her. Alice knew without asking that Molly placed all the blame on Mr. Tenpenny.

Squeezing her eyes tight, Alice forced herself to speak. "He opened his trousers."

A sharp intake of air. Exasperation, not shock, if Alice had to guess. "Made you look at his prick, did he?"

Alice nodded.

"Bastard. I'll never understand why men need to show the

world their pricks. We've all seen them." This was the best possible reaction: disgust mingled with annoyance. That was precisely how Alice might feel about the incident, if it hadn't resulted in her losing everything she had loved.

"I hadn't." She opened her eyes and turned her head to look at Molly.

"Right. Forgot about that. It must be a terrible shock for fine ladies, never to see a proper cock until they're married."

Never would Alice have guessed that she'd find something to laugh at in this situation, but laugh she did, a great wave of amusement sweeping over her until she was pressing her face into the pillow to smother the sound. "A proper cock," she repeated in between gusts of laughter.

"Or a very rude and improper one," Molly said.

"Rude indeed," Alice agreed, breathless. "Such an unprepossessing article. And he seemed so smug about the wretched thing."

Molly came over to sit on the edge of the bed, her weight dipping the mattress and causing Alice to roll slightly towards her. "What happened to get you tossed out?"

"When he took out his . . ."

"Prick," Molly supplied, which was very helpful because "member" was a good deal too dignified for the occasion.

"Well, I screamed. I ought to have . . ." Alice still didn't know what she ought to have done. Smile politely? Thank the man for his offering, the way she did when one of her brothers or nieces brought in a half-rotten turnip from the garden?

"Bugger ought to have," Molly said. "Nothing wrong with

screaming. Who knew what he meant to do with the thing? He might have meant to do more than show it to you."

Exactly. That was what Alice had feared. She was inexpressibly grateful to be understood. "I screamed, and servants came running. I went to my bedchamber, trying to avoid everybody. But he put word about that we had been . . ." She paused, hoping Molly would fill in the gaps in her vocabulary.

"Fucking?"

Well, that wasn't a word she had ever thought to hear in reference to herself. Much less would she have guessed that such a word on Molly's lips would somehow resonate deep in her own belly. "Yes, that," she managed. "And that my screams were— this was the most awkward part of the entire mortifying ordeal—"the result of pleasure."

"Oh, the shit-eating bastard."

"Precisely. My father didn't believe me, and he decided that I had to be sent from home to protect his reputation. My father is a clergyman, you know, and Mr. Tenpenny's uncle is Lord Malvern, who owns my father's living and could cast my father out on his ear if trouble got back to him." That was what had started all the trouble. Mrs. Wraxhall and Mr. Tenpenny had been among the guests at a nearby house party; Alice and her father had been invited to join the party for supper. It was the sort of invitation Alice had been accustomed to. She had worn her least shabby gown and prepared herself for an evening of conversation with another spinster or someone too tiresome for the real guests to endure. Instead she had been cornered by Mr. Tenpenny in a shadowy alcove, then dragged home by her father only to be berated and cast out. Mrs. Wraxhall had somehow gotten wind of what had actually happened, and if it hadn't been for that, Alice didn't like to think about what would have become of her.

"And now the fucker's here?" Molly's indignation somehow served to tamp down Alice's own sense of being put upon.

"He's expected tonight, I gather. I can't go downstairs."

Molly tucked one of her feet under her other leg and propped herself up on a hand. This small adjustment only lessened the distance between them by a few inches, but it seemed to Alice that it caused the temperature in the room to go up by several degrees. Suddenly she was very aware of the fact that if she moved her own hand a bit to the side, her own little finger would touch Molly's.

That little finger felt like a question that needed answering. Alice's hand was prickling with awareness, her entire being concentrated on one small digit, until the decision to move it or not move it seemed the most fundamental one of her life.

Almost without thinking, she slid her hand that final inch towards Molly's, and as soon as she felt the warm brush of skin against skin, Molly moved her own hand to cover Alice's. She could feel Molly's calluses against the places where her own calluses used to be. She could feel Molly's pulse beating against her own.

"You don't need to go downstairs," Molly said, and her voice did not sound entirely normal to Alice, which was reassuring because Alice felt nothing like normal herself. "But if you don't, people might talk about why."

"I'm sure nobody even knows that I'm here." She had done her best to fade into the wallpaper. It was a skill she had finely honed.

The mattress shifted again, and when Alice opened her eyes she saw Molly lying next to her. Their hands, still clasped, were between them.

"Here's the problem, though." Molly's voice was soft, only loud enough to be heard by someone sharing the same pillow. "This Tenpenny bastard seems just the sort of snake who would find out you were here, and then spread word that you were avoiding him because your heart was broken after he ended your affair."

Alice groaned, recognizing the truth of this. She turned to bury her face in the pillow once more.

Then came the brush of Molly's hand against her temple, sweeping a bit of hair back from her face. The gesture caught Alice by surprise. It was so gentle and tender, it felt meant for someone else entirely. Molly's warm, kind fingers seemed as out of place on Alice's head as a crown of diamonds would be. Alice didn't deserve either. She shifted away from Molly's touch.

"Hey, now," Molly whispered, evidently mistaking the cause of Alice's unease. "You've survived worse."

It was true. She had survived far worse than an evening of

awkward embarrassment. But that didn't make encountering Mr. Tenpenny any more appealing. "You're right. I'll grit my teeth and get through it."

"Bugger grit." Molly smiled her crooked smile, her lips so close to Alice's they were nearly touching. Nearly, but not quite. "We can do better than that."

Molly showed Alice exactly which seams to unpick and how they needed to be resewn.

"But—" A line appeared between Alice's eyebrows.

"Trust me."

And Alice did as she was told, as if she really did trust Molly, and wasn't that something. Molly kept expecting Alice to realize that Molly was nothing more than a street urchin with a dishonest past. Sooner or later everyone did.

"I'll be back as soon as I've dressed Mrs. Wraxhall." Molly left Alice alone, her lap covered in swathes of pale gray silk, and when she came back almost two hours later, Alice was trying on the remade gown before the looking glass.

It wasn't every woman who could make a colorless frock look like something special, but Alice managed the trick. The rest of her was pale to the point of colorlessness, from the white-blond hair that now hung loose around her shoulders, to the gray-blue eyes that regarded Molly's reflection in the looking glass. Bright fabric would wash her out, but pastels were what Mrs. Wraxhall called insipid and Molly called boring. This gown was the palest gray, and the great joke was that Alice had likely chosen it because she thought it a safe, dull, unobjectionable choice.

And so it was, if you were blind and had no taste in either gowns or women. Christ, but she looked like one of those marble statues the gentry fussed over. Every other woman would look like gaudy rubbish beside her.

"I look like a harlot."

Molly took a step closer. "Show me the harlot who wears dove-gray silk."

"You can see my breasts."

No, you really couldn't, more's the pity. The gown was depressingly modest, but if you were used to being covered chin to wrists, this was a bit of a change. Molly's alterations had only removed the length of silk gauze that served to dowdily fill in the evening gown's neckline, and then bring the waist up a crucial half inch to enhance the bustline.

"Only this morning you were telling me you don't have any, so I can't see what the fuss is." Molly came to stand behind Alice at the looking glass and tugged the bodice so it sat where it belonged. She let her hands come to rest on Alice's rib cage. Damn it if she couldn't feel Alice's heart beating, an almost frantic flutter beneath silk and skin. If she had only been looking at Alice, she might not have guessed—her expression was unruffled, her face placid and composed.

Molly slid her hands up a bit, her thumbs whispering against the bottom curve of breast, all the while keeping her eyes fixed on Alice's in the mirror. Alice met her gaze, held it, and gave a little nod.

That nod did Molly in. She hadn't been expecting anything so overt, had thought maybe they'd spend the next few days at the knife's edge between flirtation and something more. A stray touch here, a suggestive comment there, but nothing that couldn't be dismissed, forgotten, easily taken back.

She never thought they'd actually touch one another. That was the stuff of daydreams.

She could still step away. That would be safe. Molly had learned the hard way not to go to bed with employers. But Alice wasn't an employer, and more than that, Molly had the sense that they could trust one another. That they were in this together. That they were both safe.

That was a daydream too, though. If they did this, then they would do it again, and they were already too fond of one another. Going to bed with someone you were fond of was a terrible idea. You either got your heart broken or you didn't, and at the moment Molly didn't know which would be worse. She thought she could handle heartbreak, but the other thing—trying to be with a person who grew to be ashamed of herself and of Molly—seemed unbearable.

But Molly was terrible at doing the safe thing.

She skimmed her hands up to cup the slight swell of Alice's breasts, feeling her nipples pebble beneath the layers of fabric. "Just like I told you," she said, her voice little more than a whisper. "Sweet."

Alice's hands clapped over her own, not stopping Molly but holding her in place. Molly let her gaze drop from Alice's face to where their hands were joined. She leaned in, brushing a kiss against the place where Alice's neck met her shoulder, relishing the shiver that went through her body.

"I need to dress your hair," Molly said, because she didn't know what else to say, and also because as a matter of professional pride, she couldn't let Alice leave this room with her hair so plain. They only had a quarter of an hour before Alice needed to be downstairs for dinner. But Alice shifted her stance a bit, so her back was pressed against Molly's chest, and that was all the invitation Molly needed to run her fingers along the freshly tacked neckline of Alice's gown. She dipped a single finger beneath the thin linen of the chemise, but the neckline was still too damned high to get anywhere interesting.

She could feel the tiny, even stitches beneath her fingers, stitches Alice had taken because she trusted Molly to save her from the fate that awaited her downstairs.

"Sit down," she said, pressing Alice into the chair. That hair, Christ. It was usually pinned in a workaday knot, no tendrils, no curls. Molly took it down and let it slip through her fingers like water, like moonshine.

And then she got to work.

"There's nothing that can't be cured with lip rouge and strong drink," Molly said as she brushed Alice's hair for what seemed like the ninetieth time.

Alice didn't have any experience with either substance.

"I'll have to take your word for it," she said. And she would. She had put herself entirely in Molly's hands—literally and figuratively, she recalled, willing herself not to blush when Molly's eyes were on her.

She blushed anyway, and Molly's crooked smile only made her cheeks heat more furiously.

"Here's what you'll do," Molly said, the hairpin she had clenched between her teeth causing her words to take on a rakish air. "You walk into the drawing room like you're an heiress, like you're doing everybody a great favor by being there. You aren't here to wind yarn or fetch liniments for old ladies. You're here because you're young and beautiful—no, stop that, just look at yourself—and mysterious."

Alice laughed. "I'm anything but mysterious. I'm a penniless spinster with no connections. There are hundreds of women like me in every county in England."

"Not with your reputation, there aren't," Molly said, expertly twisting a lock of Alice's hair.

"My reputation," Alice repeated, taking in the meaning of what Molly said. "The only people here who I've ever met are Mrs. Wraxhall and Mr. Tenpenny. And I can only imagine what Mr. Tenpenny would say about me."

"Exactly," Molly said, as if satisfied that her pupil had caught on so quickly. "Use that."

"Use it?" Alice echoed.

"Right. So, you've spent the day helping ladies embroider cushions. Nobody would think that you were turned out of your home for a scandal. More likely, you inherited a fortune and went to live with Mrs. Wraxhall to make connections suitable to your new station, and Mr. Tenpenny hopes to marry you."

There was something about the rote precision with which she uttered those last words that made Alice narrow her eyes. "Have you been telling people that faradiddle?"

"Maybe," Molly said, her expression pure wickedness. "Servants do gossip." She twisted and pinned a few more strands of hair that somehow did not promptly tumble down, which was a feat Alice had never managed on her own. "Now for the lip rouge."

"No rouge," Alice said immediately. She could tolerate having the upper quarter of her meager bosom exposed, but lip rouge was out of the question. "And it's no use telling me that Mrs. Wraxhall wears it, because I know she does and that doesn't change anything." Mrs. Wraxhall was wealthy, married, and—more importantly than any of that—she didn't mind being the center of attention. She rather seemed to thrive on it, in fact. Alice preferred to blend into the background and manage not to embarrass herself overmuch.

"Only a little," Molly protested. "Right here." She traced her thumb slowly along Alice's lower lip. Suddenly the touch had nothing to do with lip rouge.

"No lip rouge." When Alice spoke, the pad of Molly's thumb brushed the soft, wet inside of her lip. Sparks of warmth shot through Alice's body, settling somewhere in the vicinity of her breasts, and sending a thrill of awareness somewhat lower.

"We can do it the other way, then," Molly murmured, and leaned close, brushing her own mouth against Alice's. And if Molly's thumb had produced sparks, her mouth created an inferno, burning away whatever doubts Alice had. This touch, this woman, this thing that existed between them, it was good and true and so very warm. She brought one hand up to reach for Molly's face, instinctively trying to double their points of contact. Molly's own hands were braced on the back of Alice's chair.

The brush of lips against lips turned into something more insistent, a nibbling, then a sucking. Molly's mouth was asking Alice a question, and all Alice knew was that the answer was yes.

"Yes," she said out loud.

Molly pulled back and regarded Alice carefully, her mouth twisted in that crooked, rakish smile. "That'll do very nicely." She gestured to the looking glass, and Alice saw that her lips were pink, as if she had used the dreaded rouge.

Something about her rosy lips made her look more closely at herself, really examine her gown and hair. It was her own best gown, worn at least half a dozen times already, but with Molly's alterations it looked almost fashionable. Had she seen another woman wearing such a dress, she might even have called it elegant. And her hair, even though it was dressed simply, was different enough from her usual style to make her gaze at her face in an entirely different way.

It was the face of someone who had just been kissed.

No, that was the least of what she saw in the mirror. What she saw was someone who wanted something, and who was allowed to have it. Not a person who had to pay rent for her place on earth by keeping busy, by serving others.

She could want something, and she could take it.

CHAPTER FIVE

The clock had already chimed two before Molly returned to the bedroom, her feet sore and her eyes stinging with fatigue. Mrs. Wraxhall had needed to be undressed, her hair put in curling papers, her face anointed with French creams. Then Molly had to see about a claret stain on her ladyship's green satin gown and set out tomorrow's many changes of clothing, from shoes to ear bobs and everything in between.

When she quietly pushed open the bedroom door, she expected to find Alice fast asleep, as she had been the previous night when Molly had finally collapsed into bed.

But there she was, sitting at the cramped table, pen in hand, writing by the light of a candle that had nearly burnt down. She looked up as Molly shut the door, her face arranged in an expression that gave nothing away. That, Molly guessed, was the face she used when dealing with her whoreson relations, like some poor little creature rolling up into a ball to look less interesting to a hawk.

"How was dinner?" Molly kept her voice low in case there were sleeping guests nearby, but it came out too husky and intimate.

The mask of nothingness dropped, and even in the sparse light Molly could tell that Alice was glowing. She was the brightest thing in this room, and Molly's heart skipped a beat with relief and something else entirely. "I didn't pay him the least bit of attention. Or at least I pretended not to, which amounts to much the same thing. I had other things on my mind. I suppose that was what you meant by kissing me, to provide a distraction—"

"Like hell it was," Molly protested, her hands on her hips.

"I meant that if your intention was to take my mind off the matter of Mr. Tenpenny, you succeeded."

Molly raised an eyebrow. "It wasn't that either." Alice had to know that, but if she needed reassurance, well, that didn't cost Molly a thing. "What are you writing?" Sitting up late to write a letter made no sense if you had nobody to write to.

"Oh." A faint flush crept up Alice's neck. "I wrote another fairy story for your little girl. She seemed to like the one you read her last week."

One of the reasons Molly was not only alive but also in possession of clean clothes and a full belly was that she knew how to keep a weather eye out for all possibilities. She hadn't thought there was such thing as taking Molly Wilkins by surprise.

She was surprised now.

"Thank you." She had gotten out of the habit of gratitude. What she had, she either earned or stole, and there was precious little difference between the two as far as she cared. But this, this was a gift. "Thank you," she repeated. "She'll enjoy it very much."

"I always liked making up the stories, and without my nieces . . ." Her voice trailed off.

Those bastards. "Katie and I will be glad for any of your stories. Tell me more about dinner while I help you out of that gown." It was a dirty trick and Molly knew it, even though there was scarcely any other way out of a gown like this one. Alice automatically turned her back for Molly to unwork the fastenings. Molly kept her movements brisk and efficient, flicking open buttons, unpinning hair. That much was no more than what she did for Mrs. Wraxhall. What was different was that she wasn't doing this as a servant for a master, but as a service to a friend.

As Molly performed all these familiar tasks, she asked about dinner—who sat where, how that shiteating Tenpenny bastard reacted to seeing her, whether their suspicions about Mrs. Wraxhall having a lover were founded. Alice gloried in her triumph, and a sorry thing it was that for her a triumph was breathing the same air as the man who had gotten her tossed out of her home. Molly would dearly have liked to serve him up a nasty trick.

And right as she took the last pin from Alice's hair, a plan began to form in Molly's crooked, warped brain. Oh, she really oughtn't think of anything like this, not with her position on the line, but it was just too excellent an opportunity to pass up.

But then Alice raised her arms for Molly to whisk the

gown over her head, and all her thoughts went up in a cloud of smoke.

Molly was no stranger to ladies in their chemises. Ladies in their chemises, and sometimes in nothing at all, earned Molly her daily bread.

Alice was just another lady in her chemise.

Except for the look on her face. There wasn't a hint of that bland, harmless mask. Alice's jaw was set, her chin tilted up almost defiantly.

"What's that about?" she asked, tracing Alice's jaw with her finger.

"You were right."

"It happens. What about?"

"I do like to look at you." The words came out in a jumble, Alice's voice higher than it usually was. She opened her mouth as if to say something more—Molly would have bet it was an apology—but she slammed her mouth shut. There was nothing to apologize for, and they both knew it.

Molly's breath rushed out, relief at a tension she hadn't known she was feeling. Alice wasn't going to run from this. She rested a hand on the nip of Alice's waist, only a wisp of linen in between them. "Good to know I didn't dream it up." And now her other hand was on the small of Alice's back, not so much pulling her near as letting her know that coming closer was an option if she chose to take it. She didn't want to frighten Alice off with clumsy boldness.

"I had an idea," Molly said, suspecting that more talking was going to be required before Alice was entirely at her ease. "Tenpenny is a rich man." Molly had conducted a bit of espionage belowstairs. "He came with six horses. Four hunters and two carriage horses." Even among nobs, this was extravagant. "He also brought a valet, a coachman, and a pair of grooms." The grooms and coachman would be no trouble, as they wouldn't set foot in the house beyond the kitchens. The valet was a man and could be dealt with like any other man—with a little flirtation and a lot of gin.

Alice wrinkled her brow. "No, I don't think he actually is rich. He depends on an allowance from his aunt and uncle. I overheard some ladies saying he needs to marry well." Alice had stepped closer, and now was almost in Molly's arms. Almost. "He certainly spends a great deal of money, though."

"What do you say we take some of it off his hands?" Too late, Molly realized that she had made a miscalculation. All the warmth drained from Alice's face. She was, after all, a proper lady, a clergyman's daughter for God's sake, and would not look kindly on wanton thievery. "Never mind," she said quickly, removing her hands from Alice's waist and stepping backward. "I must be off my head."

Alice opened her mouth and shut it again, then furrowed her brow, as if she were trying to work out a difficult sum. "But what would we take?"

Alice must have lost her mind. Here she was, not only condoning larceny but also offering to help. Surely this was wrong. It said so in the Bible. It said so in whatever books they wrote laws in.

But try as she might, she couldn't make herself believe

that stealing from Mr. Tenpenny was wrong. With his lies, he had ruined her reputation and gotten her cast off by her family. Wasn't the Bible filled with rules about what to do when somebody had stolen one's oxen or chickens or whatnot? Surely having one's life stolen out from under one's feet counted for more than livestock.

As for laws, it turned out that she didn't give a fig for them. They were all made up by gentlemen who didn't have to worry about having their lives come undone because one man decided to wave his prick about.

"He wore a diamond cravat pin at dinner," Alice said. She wanted that cravat pin. She wanted six cravat pins. She wanted to pave a road with cravat pins stolen from lying reprobates. She was an avenging angel, she was justice with her scales, she was going to steal a diamond.

"That's a start," Molly said, and Alice's heart soared with the thought that there was more that could be stolen, more that could be done to set things right.

"A thousand pounds," Alice said, thinking for the first time of the precise cost of her exile, measuring it not in shame and loneliness, but in shillings and pence. Naturally, mere money couldn't make up for the other things she lost—her home, her family—but it was a start. It was a necessary beginning.

"I doubt it'll fetch quite that much," Molly said. "Unless the stone is the size of a quail egg."

"No, I mean the amount my father owes me. My mother left a thousand pounds for my dowry." The word *dowry* left a bad taste in her mouth, because there had never been any question of her marriage. She would never have abandoned her siblings to her father's tyranny and it wasn't as if she had ever met a gentleman who caught her fancy.

You're more interested in bosoms.

Molly's words echoed in her ears.

"Is it yours? I mean, would a lawyer say that thousand pounds was properly yours?"

Alice wasn't certain. All she knew was that it was what her mother had wished and that her father had known it; whether she had made a will or properly settled the money was quite a closed book to her. "It hardly matters. I can't afford a lawyer to look into it."

Molly's mouth was twisted to the side in a pensive expression. "What would you do with it?"

"With a thousand pounds?" Alice knew that she could live off the interest. She could scrape by on even less. But that wasn't what she wanted. "I'd open a boarding house," she said, giving voice to an idea that had been lurking at the back of her mind for the past weeks of idleness. "I'm good at keeping house, and I think I'd find it satisfying if I were paid for my troubles."

"A boarding house," Molly repeated, and then fell silent for so long that Alice began to wonder if she thought the idea a terrible one—shabby and ungenteel and all the things Alice knew she was, deep down. Finally, Molly nodded, as if she had come to a decision. "Well, I'm for bed."

That was it? Was their discussion of thievery purely

hypothetical? What about Alice's restitution? And what about the kissing? Was there to be no more kissing? That was even more disappointing.

Molly turned her back to Alice and began wriggling out of her dress, the very picture of modesty, as if they hadn't been groping and ogling one another by turns for half the day.

"What about the, ah, cravat pin?" Alice asked, because that seemed easier to address than the kissing.

"I'll take care of that tomorrow," Molly said, as if it were an utterly commonplace errand she was planning to complete, like sewing on a boot button. "Don't worry about it." She made an attempt to wave her hand in dismissal, but her arm was still caught up in her sleeve, arresting her motion.

"For heaven's sake, let me help you," Alice said, and it came out as a scold more than an offer.

"It's all right," Molly said without turning around. "I'm used to undressing myself."

"I wasn't talking about undressing you." But she went to Molly anyway, helping tug the sleeve away from her arm. "I meant the, ah, cravat pin situation. Let me help you with that."

"I'm used to handling that sort of thing on my own too, come to think." Now the other arm was free, and Molly was shimmying out of the dress with a good deal more wiggling and bouncing than Alice could observe with equanimity. Likely Molly was using Alice's lust to distract her from jewel theft, and wasn't that something.

"Bollocks on *used to*," Alice managed to say. "Let me help."

Molly threw her dress over the back of her chair, quickly

followed by a petticoat and corset. She was standing only in her shift, and Alice's first instinct was to look away, to neatly fold the petticoat or do anything that would keep her hands busy and her eyes away from Molly's barely clad body.

Instead she stepped close, so close she could feel the warmth coming from Molly's skin. "Please," she said, tentatively touching Molly's shoulder.

"You don't know the first thing about thieving." Molly put her foot up on the chair and began rolling down one stocking, then the other. "You'd clomp around, get us sent to the gallows."

"I've never clomped in my life, I'll have you know." If Alice had known she would be spending the midnight hours proving her criminal bona fides, she might have gone to bed earlier. She was unspeakably glad that she hadn't. "I'm quite good at sneaking." She had learned the value of silence early. Silence was safety. "Besides, you have a daughter. You can't take that kind of risk." Alice had nothing, and therefore nothing to lose.

Molly regarded Alice with narrowed eyes, one hand on her hip. "All right then." Alice felt almost giddy. "But first, bed." And with that, Molly dropped onto the bed and slid under the covers.

There was to be no kissing, then. Surely Alice could live with that. She wasn't supposed to be kissing anybody anyway. Kissing was for other people. This was something she had known as a basic truth from her earliest days: so much of life was for other people. Love and safety, admiration and friendship—Alice had never had those things and hadn't wasted much time bemoaning the fact.

But now she wanted those things too. She wanted cravat pins and kisses, things that were bright and warm and hers.

Then Molly reached an arm out and patted the bed beside her. "Come on then," she said, her voice already heavy with sleep. Alice climbed into bed, resting her head on Molly's outstretched arm, settling into the space by Molly's side. They fit together like this.

Alice might have been astonished by the speed with which Molly fell asleep if she didn't recall doing the same when her days had been filled with work. Alice wasn't ready for sleep, though. Her nerves felt stretched out to the point where they vibrated with excitement. She was going to take back what was hers.

But first she pulled the quilt up to Molly's chin so she wouldn't get cold.

CHAPTER SIX

A few years of living the life of a decent, law-abiding servant had left Molly unready for the rush of mingled excitement and fear she felt upon waking. It was still dark, and Alice was still asleep, pale hair even whiter in the moonlight. Once again, one of her arms had found its way to Molly's waist as if it belonged there.

It had been a long time since Molly had wanted to touch someone so badly. It had been even longer since she wanted to be touched.

Christ, it was even longer since she had planned a robbery.

Last night she had only agreed to let Alice help in order to end the conversation. There was no possibility that a prim lady, a vicar's spinster daughter, a girl who had never been anywhere or seen anything until Mrs. Wraxhall took her in, could be trusted to properly steal a diamond.

And yet. Molly had noticed how Alice crept about as if on cat's paws, how she had a knack for entering and leaving a room without disturbing so much as the air around her. Her fingers were as nimble as any pickpocket's. And she wanted this. Molly had seen the look in her eyes, that gleam of want. Tenpenny—and her father, the lout—had hurt her, and she wanted to get back some of what was hers. This was her chance to do, to take, to earn something for herself.

If Molly managed this robbery on her own, she'd be taking that chance away from Alice. Even if she then gave Alice the cravat pin—or, rather, the proceeds from the sale of the diamond, because she doubted Alice knew how to find a fence or even a pawn shop—it wasn't the same as Alice taking it for herself.

Molly wondered whether she could teach Alice to pick a lock. Sighing, she rolled over.

Alice opened one eye, the other being hidden in the pillow. "What time is it?"

"Not yet dawn," Molly whispered, turning her head to the side. "Go back to sleep."

She didn't shut her eyes though, and neither did Molly. They had spent the entire night pressed together, and now Molly felt achingly comfortable with the rise and fall of Alice's chest, with the strands of silky moonshine hair that spread everywhere across the pillow, with the simple bodily fact of Alice's closeness.

"Thank you for helping me last night," Alice said in a sleepy voice. "With the gown and hair and everything. I felt . . ."

"Beautiful," Molly interrupted. "You were beautiful."

Alice's gaze darted off to some dark corner of the room.

"I was going to say that I felt like I belonged. Or at least that I didn't stand out awkwardly. Thank you for that."

Never had Alice heard such a fat lot of horse shite from an otherwise sensible woman. "God, I've never met one so keen on going unnoticed. You'd think you were one of those birds that looks like tree bark or what have you." So quiet, so ready to assume an air of harmless nothingness when she was so much more than that. "And why would you want to blend in with the lot of them anyway?" She was worth twenty of them. Molly tried to find words that might show Alice what she meant. "Last night you shone. You always do."

Alice returned her gaze to Molly, her eyes widening with surprise before narrowing skeptically. "I don't—"

"And if you think I'm going to spend the time until dawn making you take a compliment you can guess again." In the darkness, Molly heard Alice let out a puff of laughter that crushed whatever last bit of good judgment Molly had.

Ever so carefully, Molly shifted so she was leaning on one forearm, poised half over Alice.

Alice went still. Molly held her breath, waiting. Then Alice tilted her chin up so their lips were so close, nearly touching. "Oh?" It came out as a breath that Molly could feel on her own mouth.

And then when Molly finally dipped her head to bring her lips to Alice's, she felt Alice rising up to meet her.

Molly had tumbled her fair share of men and a couple of girls too. She was no stranger to lust or even to the stray feelings that sometimes got tangled up in lust, like those bits of rubbish that got spun into otherwise serviceable yarn, and needed to be picked out and cast aside.

But now, so close to this perfect moonlight slip of a girl, she felt like she was entirely made of those impractical bits of fluff, all woven together into something gossamer-fine and unspeakably dangerous.

One of Alice's hands was fluttering in the general neighborhood of Molly's elbow, as if it were lost and needed directions, so Molly took it and guided it to her breast. She wanted those clever hands all over her body, she wanted to taste every bit of that soft mouth.

"Oh, fff—" Molly groaned, biting back a curse as Alice's hand cupped around her breast.

"Is that all right?"

No, it was not all right. Nothing was all right. It turned out that Molly had spent her entire life wanting this woman's hand on her breast and hadn't realized it until now. "Don't stop," she managed.

Featherlight touches through her shift were only going to drive her out of her mind, though. She broke the kiss long enough to sit back and pull her shift over her head. And then, oh, the look on Alice's face, the wide-eyed wonderment and plain workaday lust. Molly thought she might burn from the heat of that gaze.

Alice was keeping her fingers tightly wrapped around the sheets, so Molly cupped her breasts in her own hands, as if she were weighing them, stroking her thumbs over the hard tips.

"I've imagined you doing that," Alice whispered, her eyes wide.

She had? "You have?" Molly had known the effect her breasts had on Alice and often felt the girl's gaze following her hotly around the room. But the idea that Alice imagined Molly touching herself wasn't even something she dared to think of. "Tell me more."

"I . . ." Alice shook her head.

"Show me, then. Show me what you did when you thought of me doing this." She lightly twisted her nipples between her thumbs and forefingers.

"Oh . . ." Alice breathed, squirming under Molly. Her hands were fisted in the sheets, as if she were afraid that if she let go, her hands might do something unspeakable. "No. You show me. Let me watch."

Molly had her hand between her legs on the next heartbeat. As if she had to be told twice. Slowly, making a bit of a show about it, she traced the seam of her sex. "Just like that, nice and easy." Beneath her, Molly felt Alice try to buck her hips, straining for contact, breasts arching up. "The only trouble," Molly said, "is that I haven't enough hands to do the thing properly."

And then Alice's clever hands were on Molly's breasts, stroking and teasing, squeezing and caressing, followed by her mouth, wet and hot and sweet. How had Molly ever thought her a shrinking violet, a meek and mild country mouse? Alice rose to every challenge; she met Molly more than halfway no matter what.

Molly felt her pleasure start to gather, to tighten into something that couldn't be stopped. A few more strokes of her finger and she burst, collapsing onto Alice's chest. She could feel the other woman's heart beating frantically, could feel the rise and fall of her chest with each shallow breath. Molly kissed her soft, parted lips before moving lower, kissing a path down to the lace trim of Alice's night rail.

Each one of Molly's kisses kindled something dreadful in Alice, something that would surely have been better left undiscovered. These touches bore no resemblance to her own solitary pleasure, carried out on the rare instances she had a bedchamber to herself. Molly was stoking a flame Alice had previously thought a mere spark, something easily dismissed and ignored, but which was now going to burn the house down if she didn't do something about it.

If she asked Molly to stop, she would. Alice knew that. The trouble was that she wanted Molly to keep doing that, keep pressing her lips to the curve of Alice's neck, keep her hand threaded in Alice's hair, keep doing those things and more. Not just this moment, not even just now, but on and on. It wasn't a safe thing to want. But Alice did want it, and that was reason enough.

Alice moaned when Molly's lips closed around her nipple through the thin linen chemise, fervently licking and sucking, and she seemed to be relishing every soft murmur she drew from Alice's lips.

"Show me," Molly said, lifting her head away from the now-wet linen. "Show me what you do when you think of me." She rucked up the hem of Alice's night rail, and when Alice felt the cool morning air between her legs, her brief wave of embarrassment was quickly displaced by the urgency of desire. Alice took the hem higher, until it was under her chin and she was fully exposed, on display, for Molly's hot, seeking gaze. "Oh, God, look at you," Molly said. She skimmed her hands down Alice's sides, from ribs to waist to hips, as if Alice were a rare and precious thing.

With one hand still on her hip, Molly used the other hand to stroke between Alice's legs. "Is this how you like it?" She brushed fingers across Alice's tender skin, so lightly, nothing more than a whisper of a touch, skimming again and again over the place where all her want was concentrated.

Alice stifled a cry. That was most definitely not how she touched herself. She was more given to efficient, workman-like self-pleasure, nothing like this torture.

"Or is it like this?" Now Molly's fingers were parting her. Another flush of embarrassment, quickly dismissed as trivial. "Maybe like this?"

Now there was a finger inside her, which was a strange thing to contemplate. "That's not how I do it," Alice whispered. It had never seemed quite necessary—she could get the job done without that, after all.

"Do you want me to stop?"

"No," Alice whispered. "Please don't stop." She really didn't know what would become of her if Molly stopped. Perhaps she'd crumble into a heap of ash. Perhaps she'd cry. Who knew? She hoped she didn't find out.

Molly didn't stop. Instead she did something magical with her hand, so that she was touching inside Alice and also stroking that sensitive place outside with those infuriatingly featherlight touches. And then—oh—she bent her head to Alice's breast and drew a nipple into her mouth, this time without the linen between them.

Alice was dimly aware that she was arching her back, trying to press into Molly's hand. She was vaguely conscious of the stream of whispered blasphemy that was pouring from her mouth. But compared to the twin sorcery of Molly's hand and mouth, none of that signified.

Her climax felt wrenched out of her, terrible and miraculous all at once, wracking her body with an intensity one usually associated with disaster—carriage accidents and hurricanes.

"Molly," she said. "Molly."

"I'm here," Molly said, holding her tight.

CHAPTER SEVEN

"You're a cuddler," Molly said, after they had dozed. "You chased me into this corner of the bed and gave me no quarter until you had your arm around me." Alice moved to pull her arm back, but Molly grabbed it, fixing it in place on her own waist. "Nah, I like it. I'd have shoved you off if I didn't."

"It's true." The first rays of sunlight were glinting off Alice's loose hair. She stretched an arm lazily over her head. "I suppose I ought to get a cat."

"I don't think cats go in much for cuddles." Not the ones Molly had known, at least, but they had mostly been a hungry, rat-obsessed bunch. Perhaps ladies' cats had different priorities.

"Maybe a dog, then," Alice said, yawning.

"Or a person," Molly suggested.

"A person?"

Molly cringed at her own stupidity. "You seem to be doing all right in the bed with me, I mean to say. We could keep on doing this, if you like."

Well, that woke her up. Molly watched in chagrin as all the sleepiness drained from Alice's face. "But only for the remainder of the house party," she said, her voice tight. "After that we'll have our separate rooms."

"It doesn't need to be that way."

Alice, her face once again set in that bland and harmless mask, glanced away to some point over Molly's naked shoulder. "I doubt that even Mrs. Wraxhall would tolerate this kind of carrying on under her own roof."

Was that what they were doing? Carrying on? Molly had thought it was more, something, unlike every bloody connection she had ever made, that might last longer than the other person had use for Molly, that might last longer than it took for the other person to find out what Molly really was.

She climbed out of bed and pulled a fresh shift out of the clothes press. Last night's was God knew where. "It's cold as a witch's tit," she said briskly. Alice still hadn't gotten out of bed, and Molly hardly dared look for fear her expression would give her stupidity away. "You ought to get dressed before you catch your death, and then I'll show you how to pick a lock."

"I don't believe you'll need to teach me how to do that," Alice said slowly.

"Having second thoughts about tolerating crime? You seemed keen enough on it last night." Molly ought to be glad. She had no business risking her position. "Just as well, I suppose."

"What?" Alice seemed genuinely bewildered. "Of course I was. And I am. What I meant was that I know how to pick a lock."

Molly raised an eyebrow. "And how the devil did you learn to do that?"

"One of my brothers used to get locked in the cupboard as a punishment, and I would let him out after my father had drunk himself into oblivion."

A real charmer, the vicar. Molly only raised an eyebrow.

"I used to sometimes pay the housemaid's wages out of the strongbox after my father had fallen asleep," Alice continued. "Or I would unlock the pantry to get bits of food."

Bits of food? The way she described it, the vicarage sounded as bad as Newgate. "What do you use? Hairpins? That was what people always tried first, which was perfectly fine, except—"

"A pair of my longest embroidery needles."

Twenty minutes later, Alice, using fearsome needles that looked like small stilettos more than the sort of thing a lady would use to produce cushions for the front parlor, locked and unlocked the door to their room, her own traveling case, and Mrs. Wraxhall's jewel box.

"Well, I daresay you'll be able to manage Tenpenny's toilette case."

They settled it between them. Molly would distract Tenpenny's valet while Alice took the cravat pin. Then Alice would spend the rest of the day downstairs with the ladies and gentlemen, where she belonged, and Molly would try t

get used to the idea that she was about to become nothing more than a tawdry memory.

Alice did not think it at all likely that she would develop an appetite for further crime. When she stepped into Mr. Tenpenny's bedchamber, she expected to be immediately hauled away by thief-takers and magistrates. Instead, it was dark and quiet, the curtains drawn and the fire banked. The pounding of her heart was the loudest thing in the room. She took a deep breath that did nothing to steady her nerves.

Then she pretended that she was at the vicarage, pilfering a bit of bread from the pantry. This was only different in scale, really. Instead of bringing her brother the food he was denied because of their father's tyranny, she was taking Mr. Tenpenny's diamond to reclaim the life that was snatched from her. She had never *not* stolen—scraps of food to give to the poor, money for the servants' wages, little bits and pieces to make things right. She had always thought it a necessary part of living in her father's house—he didn't have the moral fortitude to do what was needful, so she did it.

Today would be the first time she had taken for herself.

But it wasn't only for herself. It was also for Molly. This was a joint venture. They were splitting the proceeds: half would go for Molly to put aside for Katie, and the other half would go for Alice to hire a small house where she could take in lodgers.

It seemed a waste to set up two separate households

when they could get by more cheaply together, though. Neither of them was afraid of hard work, and with a bit of economy they could live quite decently and still put money aside. Molly would be able to have Katie with her every day, rather than waiting days and weeks between short visits. Perhaps she could be induced to give up the relative security of her post with Mrs. Wraxhall to run a boarding house with Alice. They could share the work and the profits, which seemed a very sensible and efficient arrangement.

Alice knew she was lying to herself. Her interest in sharing a house, a bed, with Molly had nothing to do with economy. Seeing Molly had become the high point of Alice's day. Molly's casual profanity, Molly's swaggering walk, Molly's crooked smile—all those were somehow the precise shape of some emptiness in Alice's heart. What had happened last night in bed was only part of it—a crucial part, without a doubt—but only a part.

She dragged her thoughts back to the present. Scanning the room, she found the gentleman's toilette case sitting on the dressing table. In her pocket were embroidery needles of a few different sizes; it was the one suited for lacework that fit into the miniature keyhole. Still imagining that she was picking the pantry lock, she put her ear to the case and adjusted the needle until she felt the inner workings fall into place.

And then there it was, the lock was open. When she eased back the lid, the contents of the box gleamed in the faint light. There were a few golden guineas, an array of shirt studs, and an old-fashioned watch fob, but amidst all that sparkle and shine, she saw no cravat pin. He must be wearing it. She hadn't thought he'd be so vulgar as to wear such a bauble during the day, but perhaps men who exposed themselves to unwilling women weren't to be relied on as models of gentlemanly propriety.

She could take the shirt studs, but they were nothing compared to the diamond. She wasn't going to commit a felony for twenty pounds' worth of brass.

Resigned, she closed the lid and once again used the needle, this time to lock the box again.

No sooner had she silently dropped the needle back into her pocket when she heard the sound of a door opening. She spun on her heel, only to find Mr. Tenpenny standing in the doorway.

"What do we have here?" His voice was every bit as greasy and insinuating as it had been the day she had met him. "I daresay Mrs. Wraxhall will be charmed to know her protégée has been lying in wait in a gentleman's bedchambers. This sort of gossip is just the sort of thing to liven up a house party."

Alice's mouth went dry with dread and unchecked fear. But then she saw the sparkle of the diamond cravat pin below Mr. Tenpenny's chin.

The world suddenly divided into things that mattered and things that did not. On the former list was stolen jewels and Molly Wilkins. On the latter list was whatever claptrap Mr. Tenpenny chose to spread about.

He couldn't harm her any more than he already had, so he was free to run his mouth as much as he pleased, as far as she cared.

But how to get that pin? She tried to imagine what Molly would do in her shoes. And when the idea finally clicked in her mind, she could hardly stop from laughing.

"Oh, how embarrassing," she said, consciously adopting the contrite tone she always used to placate her father. "But I hardly knew how else to approach you."

"To approach me," Mr. Tenpenny repeated with a look of lecherous triumph.

"I was so glad when I learned that you were to be a guest at Eastgate Hall." She cast her eyes down, focusing all her attention on a swirl in the plush carpet beneath her feet rather than on the man standing before her. "So very glad." She cast a shy look at his face, then back at the carpet. "I felt so very silly after what happened at my father's house this summer, and I wanted a chance to tell you so myself." Now she looked up again, and deliberately, slowly smoothed the bodice of her gown.

Because when she had asked herself what Molly would do in this situation, the answer had been as clear as if Molly were here to whisper it laughingly in her ear: she would play the coquette and use Tenpenny's pride and weakness against him.

"Is that so?" Mr. Tenpenny took a step closer, and Alice willed herself not to step away. If all else failed, she had that needle in her pocket and wouldn't hesitate to use it.

Alice, one hand firmly gripping that needle, reached up and stroked the lapel of Mr. Tenpenny's coat.

"A minx, aren't you? I knew it. All that coyness the last time was just meant to pique my interest, I daresay."

Alice felt very bad for the ladies who had looked forward to seducing Mr. Tenpenny if the man could not tell a woman's shriek of horror from flirtatious coyness. She made a noncommittal murmur and slid her hand to the knot of his cravat. Then, just as he bent his head, presumably to kiss her with that loathsome mouth, she plucked the pin out of his cravat.

For a moment she thought of running. She could, she supposed. Would Horace Tenpenny admit to having been robbed by an insignificant spinster? He might rather lose his diamond than become a laughingstock.

There was another way, though. A smile spread across her face when she realized it.

"What the hell do you think you're doing?" Mr. Tenpenny asked, only just now comprehending what had happened.

"You owe me this." Her voice had all the conviction her father's had always held from the pulpit. It was because she was speaking the truth. He did owe her this.

"You compromised me. You ruined my reputation. If my father were another sort of man altogether, he would have demanded that you marry me. He would have written to that wealthy aunt of yours and we would have been married by Michaelmas." Thank God he hadn't. At the time, Alice might have even been grateful for the match, relieved not to have been abandoned by her family.

Mr. Tenpenny made a reach for the cravat pin, but Alice took a step back.

"No, no. You're going to listen to me. You wriggled out of

a terrible marriage that day. Imagine, a man like you, saddled with a penniless wife like me. The only reason you escaped was that my father is as much of a villain as you are. But he isn't here today. It's just me, and I have nothing to lose. All I have to do is open my mouth and scream."

"I'll tell everyone you were in my room waiting for me," he scoffed. "Nobody would think I would seduce such a one as you."

"Half this house party thinks I'm an heiress. A very boring heiress, hardly the type to seduce anybody. However, they'd quite think you capable of seducing me to force a marriage, I think. Mrs. Wraxhall has some influence. She'd demand that you marry me and wouldn't hesitate going to your aunt and uncle to insist that you cooperate. And, Mr. Tenpenny, I don't think you can afford to do without your aunt's money any more than you can afford to marry a penniless wife."

His face was a very satisfying shade of purple. "This is extortion."

Alice considered this. "Or blackmail. I can never remember which is which. Whatever the case, you'll let me have your cravat pin as a payment for letting you escape from a very improvident marriage." She could almost hear the gears of his sad little mind turning as he considered her offer.

"Fine," he said, his teeth gritted. "Get out of my room, you—"

Alice had slipped out before he could finish the sentence.

When Alice swept into their shared bedchamber, Molly knew straightaway that she had been successful. She fairly glowed. If this was what jewel theft did to a girl, it was a wonder it wasn't more common.

But Molly knew it wasn't the diamond that made Alice look like she had beams of light stuck under her skin, but rather the fact that she had taken back what was hers.

"I've got it," Alice said, holding out the cravat pin.

Molly scarcely paid the jewel any attention, instead pulling Alice into an embrace. Their hearts were both racing. "Did everything go as planned?"

"No," Alice said, the sound muffled in Molly's hair. "He found me. I made him let me have it."

That changed things. Molly had planned to hide the pin among her belongings—sewn into the hem of her skirt or the boning of her corset—until they returned to London. But now she'd have to get rid of that diamond in case Tenpenny decided to summon a magistrate and have Alice arrested. Even if she knew a pawnbroker in Norfolk, she'd hardly want to sell the diamond so close to where it had been stolen. No, she needed to go back to London now and do this thing safely.

"What's wrong?" Alice asked, leaning back to peer searchingly at Molly's face.

"No time to explain." There came the old, familiar fear of being caught, hanged, transported. "Give me the diamond so I can sell it."

Alice handed it over without hesitation. "You can't just leave, though. You'll lose your place."

She might, if it came to that. But here they were, with a stolen diamond on them, and a mean-spirited man who might do God only knew what. Even if the worst happened and she got sacked, she'd still have half the worth of the diamond.

"Thank you," she said, pressing her lips to Alice's for a kiss that was too hurried to mean anything.

CHAPTER EIGHT

Molly didn't return that night. When the sun rose the following morning and Molly still wasn't there, Alice started to worry. She had told Mrs. Wraxhall—who had been overflowing with apologies that she had inadvertently subjected Alice to Mr. Tenpenny's company during the house party—that Molly was ill, but she couldn't keep up that pretense forever. Besides, somebody must surely have seen Molly leave. She couldn't have walked to—Alice suddenly realized she had no idea where Molly planned to go. She felt utterly stupid for having let Molly go without having asked. At first, she thought Molly meant to sell the jewel in Norwich, but perhaps she intended to travel to London. In that case she couldn't possibly return until tomorrow at the earliest. And she needn't bother coming back, because there would be no job waiting for her, not after Mrs. Wraxhall inevitably realized that Molly wasn't in bed. Likely Alice would be turned off as well, after Mrs. Wraxhall discovered that she had lied about Molly's illness.

Those were relatively minor concerns, compared to the dawning certainty that Molly was not coming back. What if Molly were no different from Alice's father and sister, willing to cast Alice off as a bad bargain? Molly had given Alice no reason to think so, but Alice couldn't silence the whisper that she was worth less than a diamond. That whisper had been with her for as long as she could remember, and she had precious little evidence that she might be worth even more than a hairpin, let alone a diamond cravat pin.

That next morning, with still no word from Molly, Alice packed her valise and knocked on the door to Mrs. Wraxhall's bedchamber. The lady was sitting at her dressing table, arranging her hair as best she could without a lady's maid.

"Alice!" she exclaimed, turning to face the door. "What on earth are you doing with your valise?"

"Ma'am, I'm afraid I lied when I said that Molly was ill. The truth is that she had to leave to dispatch an errand for me, and she hasn't yet returned. It was quite wrong of me to ask her to do this, and I take full responsibility. Please don't give her the sack."

"The sack? What on earth are you talking about? What errand? Alice, you're as white as a sheet."

"I can't tell you about the errand, only that it's my fault."

Mrs. Wraxhall opened her mouth as if to ask further questions, and then snapped it shut again. Instead, she took her coin purse out of her dressing table drawer. "How much do you need to get wherever you're going?"

"I don't know where I'm going. I thought you'd want me to leave, so I ought to be prepared."

"Of course. The last time you were turned out, you hardly had enough time to grab so much as a clean shift. I have no intention of turning out either you or Molly. She's worked for me for several years, and never once have I had the least reason not to trust her. Quite the contrary, in fact. She helped me at a time when I thought I was beyond help. So I have to believe that if she saw fit to deceive me, she had a reason she thought worthy, and a person for whom she was willing to risk her position. If that person were her daughter, I feel certain that she would have told me herself. That leads me to believe that she has another person she feels strongly about, and the fact that she told you the nature of her errand suggests that you are that person. No, you don't need to confirm. Just tell me what you need."

"What I need?" Alice echoed, stunned.

"What you want, if you prefer."

What she wanted was for Molly to return, for Molly to be safe. But there was no way to ensure that. Either Molly would return or she wouldn't. All Alice could do was wait. But while she was waiting, perhaps there was something else she could do. "I want to go to the vicarage at Barton St. Mary."

Mrs. Wraxhall raised her eyebrows. "To burn it down, I hope?" she asked coolly. "Perhaps smash its windows?"

Alice smiled despite herself. "To get what's mine," she said.

"Do let me send you in my carriage," Mrs. Wraxhall said. "I'd be honored."

Alice patted the pocket where she kept the coins Molly

had gotten for selling the handkerchiefs. "I need to do this on my own."

Molly thought Alice was worth something. But Alice didn't believe it herself, and she didn't think she could manage so much as a friendship if she doubted that. She wasn't sure how to go about changing her own mind, but she knew she had to start at Barton St. Mary.

The cart left her off at the bottom of the lane that led to the vicarage. The oak trees had been heavy with leaves when she had last seen them, but now they were bare, spindly branches shaking in the wind. Alice drew her pelisse tighter around her. That was something else that was different—she had been poor and shabby, friendless and scared when she had left this place.

She was still poor, but not shabby. Perhaps not friendless. And now that she thought of it, she wasn't scared. A scared Alice would never have dared come back here.

The door was answered by a housemaid Alice had never seen before, a painfully thin child of at most twelve, wearing what Alice recognized as one of her own old frocks that had been relegated to the rag bin some time ago. It was hardly a surprise that Alice's father hadn't been able to keep their old maid without Alice around to do half the work and secretly supplement her wages. This child had likely come from the workhouse. She had shadows under her eyes and a smudge on one cheekbone that could either be dirt or a fading bruise. Alice frowned.

"I'm here to see the vicar," Alice said. She glanced around the hall. It was dirty. Nobody had cleaned the windows or dusted the woodwork since she left. "You may tell him Miss Stapleton is here."

The girl's eyes widened in what was probably a mix of fear and surprise, but she scampered off, leaving Alice to wait in the hall. Alice worried that the child would be punished as the deliverer of unwelcome news, but there came no raised voices nor the sound of objects being flung against the wall. She was seized with the realization that this house was no place for a child: not a waif from the workhouse, not the motherless children of the vicar, nobody. That housemaid didn't deserve this, and neither had Alice. The hunted look she had seen on the little housemaid's face had been familiar enough from her brothers and sisters, and on her own reflection in the looking glass.

As if by instinct, she turned towards the looking glass that had always hung in the hall, and nearly stepped back in surprise.

She was the finest thing in this sad room. Her hair was clean and tidy, despite the cart ride. Her pelisse and bonnet were new and fashionable, despite being plain. The face that looked back at her was the same face she seen in the mirror at Eastgate Hall, Molly's gaze warm and appreciative on her. She had spent three months living soft and eating well, but she had also spent those three months not being afraid. She had been treated kindly and with respect; she had been appreciated.

She took a deep breath. She could do this. She didn't wait for the maid to return but went directly to her father's study and prepared to demand what was hers.

It took Molly half a day to find the man she was looking for.

"I'm not a fucking fence, Mol." Jack Turner was scowling, so maybe nothing much had changed despite the fact that he was now living in a fine house in a respectable part of town. Jack had been the one to get Molly her place as a scullery maid when her mother had wandered off permanently and Molly found herself without anywhere to go. Jack had been a footman then, and later a valet, which were facts it was hard to remember when she saw him in this prettily papered study.

"You really can't talk that way to a lady," said the other man in the room. He was handsome, every bit as pretty as the wallpaper and about twice as grand as the house itself. She'd dearly like to know how Jack Turner came to keep this kind of company, but that would have to wait.

"I'm really not a la—" she started to protest.

"I beg your pardon, Miss Wilkins," Jack said with exaggerated courtesy and a sardonic smile that was meant for the gentleman, "but I'm not a fucking fence."

"I don't need you to sell it, Jack." As if Molly couldn't find her own fence. "I need you to make sure we don't hang for taking it."

"Oh, God, there's a 'we,'" Jack groaned. "I should have known. Who are you caught up with? Tell me it's not Brewster's gang, because I have no pull left in that quarter."

"It's not like that! She's . . . good. The man we took the diamond from, he harmed her and this is . . ." What was the word Jack used to use? "Restitution."

Jack buried his face in his hands and mumbled something that sounded like, "I've created a monster."

The blond gentleman cleared his throat. "Usually what Jack does at this point is find what information he can on the, ah, other party, so he can blackmail the man into compliance. What's his name?"

"Horace Tenpenny."

The two men exchanged a glance. "Tenpenny," Jack repeated.

"Do you think he's the same Tenpenny who hasn't been paying his servants?" the other man asked. "Because it sounds like this isn't his lucky day at all."

Molly watched as a rare smile spread across Jack's face.

"It'll be a pleasure to assist you, Miss Wilkins," the blond one said.

Alice knew her father couldn't have gotten smaller or frailer in the few months since she had been gone, but he seemed diminished. She could not say she was sorry.

"What are you doing here?" he growled by way of greeting. He didn't offer her a seat and that was just as well, because Alice had no intention of sitting. The chairs were probably filthy anyway without her around to polish them.

"I've been thinking about your expenditures," Alice said. "You get two hundred pounds a year from this living. You spend next to nothing on wages or upkeep to the house. You give nothing to charity. I spent thirty pounds a year on housekeeping. You haven't had any school fees to pay in ages.

Even if you paid fifty pounds a year to the wine merchant"—
she cast a disparaging glance at the empty brandy bottle that
sat on the corner of his desk—"that ought to leave at least
another fifty. So where does it go?"

"You traveled a hundred miles to ask me impertinent
questions about my—"

She held up a hand. "No, I came to ask you whether it's
gambling or blackmail. Because if it's neither, then you must
have money saved, and I'm not leaving without part of it, or
at the very least a promissory note."

"How dare—"

She held up her hand again. "Really, Father, I've had a
lifetime of shouting. And what you don't seem to realize is
that by casting me out you've given me the whip hand. You're
a clergyman, for goodness' sake. Throwing your daughter out
onto the street after she was accosted by a man—"

"Accosted by a man! That's what you call throwing yourself at a man like that?"

For half a heartbeat, she wondered if he actually believed that. Then she decided it didn't matter because he
didn't matter: she already knew he had neither loyalty to
nor affection for her, and she was content to return the
compliment. "Yes, Father. I call it that because that's precisely what it is. And it's precisely what everyone else will
think when I tell them." She wasn't entirely sure about this.
The sad fact was that women were seldom believed in these
situations. But she was willing to call her father's bluff. "To
be perfectly clear, I plan to tell everyone—including Lord
Malvern—that you threw me out after Mr. Tenpenny at-

tempted to assault me. I'll do it in the kindest possible way, you understand, warning ladies not to let themselves be approached by him, counseling mothers not to let him dance with their daughters. They'll listen to me, because I'm the very picture of respectable spinsterhood. I'll leave your name out of my story if you give me my dowry."

"This is blackmail."

"I truly don't care what you call it, so long as you give me my money."

When Alice had arrived at the vicarage, she hadn't been certain whether her plan would work. She supposed it was possible her father really had drunk all his income or lost it at the card table. But she knew she had to try, to let her father know that he was in her power. Still, she had to school her face into an expression of indifference when her father brought a bankbook out from his desk and handed her a draft for fifty pounds.

"And the rest?" she asked.

"I'll give you fifty pounds next year as well," he said.

"You'll make it out as an annuity. Fifty pounds annually, and then the balance of a thousand pounds to be paid on your death." She nearly asked for interest. "I'll take a promissory note to that effect, please. And," she added, inspired, "understand that I'll have my eyes on you. You'll hire a proper servant—not an impressionable child—and you'll pay her wages and treat her well. If I hear about any of your servants having so much as a paper cut, I'll be at your bishop's doorstep within the hour, and if the bishop doesn't act promptly, I'll come here myself. You'd much prefer the bishop," she added darkly, in precisely the tone she had heard Molly use when scolding the young man in the street. "Do you understand me?"

She wasn't even surprised when her father assented almost meekly.

She left the house with fifty pounds, a promissory note, and an underfed housemaid.

Chapter Nine

The problem with having spirited away the housemaid was that Alice didn't know where to go. She could hardly return to Eastgate Hall with a scrawny urchin in tow—Mrs. Wraxhall was kind, but she was not the mistress of Eastgate Hall—but no more could she have left the girl in her father's keeping. The girl needed feeding, however, so they walked to the nearest inn.

While the child—Patience—ate a shocking quantity of bread and cheese, and Alice had a medicinal quantity of sherry, Alice formulated a plan. She dashed off a note to Mrs. Wraxhall, assuring her she was well, but in possession of a child who needed bathing and looking after, and that if Mrs. Wraxhall would be so kind as to send Alice's belongings to—

That was where Alice's plan got a little hazy. The London house was closed up, empty except for those servants who had no family to visit during their holiday. Alice could afford one night at this inn, a new frock for Patience, and then the stagecoach journey back to London, but where would she go? And how would Molly know where to find her?

There really was only one answer. There was only one place in the world where Alice knew Molly would return. Part of her wanted to make Molly see her out. That way if Molly wanted to abscond with the diamond, then Alice would never need to know about it. Instead she could remember the way Molly had looked at her and know that even for a short time, Molly had wanted her, had valued her, no matter what happened afterward.

But that was cowardice. Not only cowardice, but an insult to both Molly and herself. Alice had to have faith that Molly would keep her word, that she valued Alice more than she valued a diamond pin.

Alice finished writing the rest of the letter.

It was evening the next day when they arrived in London, and it took quite a bit of winding through unfamiliar streets before Alice found the house where Molly's little girl boarded.

Mrs. Fitz, carrying Katie on her hip, remembered Alice from her visit last month, and let her into the tiny sitting room.

"Thank you," Alice said. "Am I correct that you let rooms? My maid and I need to board somewhere for a fortnight, and the friend I had been living with is in the country."

The older woman looked at her shrewdly, taking in the fine wool of her gown and the kid leather of her boots, then examining Patience, who had been scrubbed, combed, and dressed in a clean frock. "You can have my spare room for two shillings a week, supper with me and Katie included."

In the stagecoach from Norfolk, Alice had studied advertisements for boarding houses and knew that this price was on the steep side, but not quite highway robbery, so she assented.

"Just sit there while I fetch you some tea," Mrs. Fitz said, gesturing to a chair next to the fire. "Your maid can make up your bed."

"I can hold Katie, if you like," Alice offered.

"Thank you, my dear," Mrs. Fitz said. "She's just at the age where she can't be let alone for a minute."

The girl came to Alice willingly, but seemed more interested in untying Alice's bonnet ribbons than in anything else. Her progress was impeded by something she was clutching in her hand. It was a piece of white linen, or at least it had been white at some point but now was gray with grime. But beneath the dirt, Alice could make out flowers that looked impossibly familiar.

"She won't let me take it away to wash," Mrs. Fitz said, poised in the doorway. "Even though she has four just like it, that's the one she wants. She sleeps with it clutched in her hand."

"Let me see that," Alice asked, her voice strained. This couldn't be what she thought it was. Molly had sold her handkerchiefs over a month ago and had given her the proceeds.

"Elf in tree," Katie said firmly, not letting go of the linen but letting Alice look at it. It was indeed one of the handkerchiefs Alice had embroidered, the one with the elf in the cherry tree. Alice's mind reeled. Molly had lied about selling them and must have given Alice her own precious coins.

"Here's your tea," Mrs. Fitz said upon returning to the sitting room. "Goodness, miss, have you taken a turn?"

"Just a bit of air," Alice managed, "and I'll be quite all right."

Molly was bone-tired when she turned the corner onto Mrs. Fitz's street. She had sold the diamond and given the proceeds to Jack for safekeeping. Then she had returned to Eastgate Hall, only to find that Mrs. Wraxhall and Alice weren't there. The butler, after regarding Molly's dusty and rumpled clothing and noting that it was highly unorthodox for a lady's maid not to know such pertinent information as the whereabouts of her employer, told her that a letter had arrived from Mr. Wraxhall, and within the hour Mrs. Wraxhall had left with her servants to meet his ship in Dover. So back Molly went to London. She'd pop in to give a kiss to Katie and then go to Mrs. Wraxhall's house, if the woman was even there yet—not that she'd have a job anymore, but she needed to find Alice and let her know the money was waiting for her. She told herself that what came after that didn't matter: Alice was free to do as she pleased. The fact that it had evidently pleased all Molly's previous lovers to vanish from her life after they had done with her had no bearing on the matter. Alice was different.

Molly snorted at her own stupidity. Alice was different all right. She was decent and kind and would be ashamed of herself for having shared a bed and a felony with a woman who knew how to fence stolen jewels and launder the proceeds.

She frowned when she approached Mrs. Fitz's stoop. Someone was sitting there. Really, this was not the kind of neighborhood where she expected women to be lounging around in doorways. At least, not women in gray pelisses. Her eyes went wide.

She ran the rest of the way.

"What are you doing here?" Molly demanded. "You're supposed to be in Dover." Before she could think better of it, she had clasped Alice's hands and drew her to her feet.

"I'm getting the money from my father." Alice squeezed Molly's hands. "He's returning the money that my mother meant me to have. I'll get fifty pounds a year."

"What?" Molly reeled but didn't let go of Alice. "How?"

"I was quite threatening. You'd have been proud."

Where on earth was the shy, self-effacing girl who had come to London a few months ago? "You've gotten quite good at blackmailing people."

Alice let out a shaky laugh. "I'm not letting anyone treat me like I'm not worthwhile anymore. I deserve better. I have what's rightfully mine and I'm going to live the life that I choose."

"And you came here to tell me." It was . . . fine. Molly told herself that she didn't want more. If Alice wanted to go be the fine lady she was, then that was only right and proper. "You'll also have the money from the diamond. That'll be enough to set you up nicely." She tried to let go of Alice's hands but Alice's grip was too strong.

"Half the money from the diamond," Alice corrected. "And I didn't come to tell you. I came to see—" She sucked in a breath and Molly found that she was doing the same. "I came to see if you'd like to set yourself up too. I mean, with me. Despite what you think, I expect Mrs. Wraxhall isn't going to sack you for this. But I thought that maybe you'd want to try to figure something out with me? It doesn't have to be a boarding house. Whatever it is, Katie would come, of course. It could be—"

"I'd love to run a boarding house with you. Or anything you liked. Anything, Alice. I was trying to tell you that the other day."

"I know that now, but I just couldn't make myself believe it was possible." She pulled Molly a bit closer so the brims of their bonnets were nearly touching. "You've made me feel like I deserve good things. And you're the best thing of all."

Molly didn't go in much for tears, but she was crying now and there was no use pretending otherwise.

EPILOGUE

One year later

The calluses had returned to Alice's fingers, and her hands were a bit red from the harsh soap she used to scrub the stairs. At the end of a day of cooking, cleaning, and looking after Katie, she and Molly collapsed wearily onto the bed in their little room at the top of the house.

Alice had never been happier.

The winter was bitterly cold, but inside the boarding house it was warm. They spent too much on coal, because nobody was getting chilblains in any establishment Alice ran. It was Saturday, so after supper Alice had collected the coming week's rent from their lodgers and was counting it out on the kitchen table. She liked to see the rent, touch each coin with her fingers, as if to prove that she had earned that money with her own work. And she had the further satisfaction of knowing that she was doing something good: their boarding house offered safe and clean rooms to women. When a woman came to the door and looked hungry and desperate, Molly lied outright about the cost of a bed and offered it for a penny a night.

The kettle whistled, so Alice rose from the table and set about making two cups of tea. By the time she finished, Molly had come in from feeding the hens and wrapped her arms around Alice's middle. She mumbled something that sounded like "bollocks on this weather" into Alice's neck.

"We're in the kitchen," Alice protested, trying to sound stern and failing utterly.

"I'm going to do filthy things to you in the kitchen. Right next to that nice hot stove."

Alice snorted. "Right now what you're going to do is sit next to that stove and warm yourself." She loosened Molly's grip with the intention of turning to face her.

"No," Molly wailed, clinging onto her like a limpet. "You're so warm. Don't let go of me. I love you. Don't you love me too much to let me freeze?"

Laughing, Alice managed to get Molly closer to the stove. "I do love you. And you can do whatever you like to me later," she whispered.

Molly pulled back, raising an eyebrow, and Alice felt an answering warmth. "That a promise?"

"Always," Alice whispered, brushing her lips against Molly's temple.

**Keep reading for an excerpt from
Cat Sebastian's latest full-length novel,**

A DUKE IN DISGUISE

One reluctant heir

If anyone else had asked for his help publishing a naughty
novel, Ash would have had the sense to say no. But he's never
been able to deny Verity Plum. Now he has his hands full il-
lustrating a book and trying his damnedest not to fall in love
with his best friend. The last thing he needs is to discover he's
a duke's lost heir. Without a family or a proper education, he's
had to fight for his place in the world, and the idea of it—and
Verity—being taken away from him, chills him to the bone.

One radical bookseller

All Verity wants is to keep her brother out of prison, her
business afloat, and her hands off Ash. Lately it seems she's
not getting anything she wants. She knows from bitter experience that she isn't cut out for romance, but the more time
she spends with Ash, the more she wonders if maybe she's
been wrong about herself.

One disaster waiting to happen

Ash has a month before his identity is exposed, and he
plans to spend it with Verity. The longer they explore their
long-buried passion, the harder it becomes for Ash to face
the music. Can Verity accept who Ash must become, or will
he turn away the only woman he's ever loved?

Available now from Avon Impulse!

CHAPTER ONE

Ash knew all too well that there were two varieties of pleasure in life. The first included art, fine weather, good company, and all the rest of the world's benign delights. A man could hold these pleasures at arm's length, appreciate them with the proper detachment, and not mourn their absence overmuch. But a fellow could be ruined by overindulgence in the second category of pleasure: rich food, strong drink, high stakes gaming.

Verity Plum belonged squarely in the latter category.

For all she was one of Ash's dearest friends and one of the few constants in his life, for all she and her brother were now the closest thing to family that he had in this country, being near her was a pleasure he meted out for himself in small doses, like the bottle of French brandy he kept in his clothes press, lest he succumb to the emotional equivalent of gout.

As a very young man he had compared Verity, pen in

hand and smudged spectacles balanced on the tip of her nose, to a bird diligently building a nest. Ten years later he knew it to have been the romantic delusion of a youthful idiot not to have straightaway seen the bloodlust lurking behind the spectacles; she bore more in common with a hawk picking the meat from its prey's bones than with a songbird collecting twigs and leaves.

He had arrived in town late the previous night, when the house was dark and the doors locked. He let himself in using the latchkey Mr. Plum had given him ten years ago and which he still carried on a string around his neck. Weary from the journey from Portsmouth and loath to wake the household, he left his satchel at the foot of the stairs, climbed up to the spare room, and went promptly to sleep. When he woke, a cup of coffee and a buttered roll sat on the table beside his bed, and his satchel rested on a hard-backed chair, which meant somebody at least knew he had arrived. Could be Verity, could be Nate, could be old Nan, who still came in every morning to do the cleaning. Could be a stray vagabond off the streets or one of the impecunious writers who often made their home in the garrets of the Holywell Street premises of Plum & Company, Printers and Booksellers.

Now he cast his gaze around Verity's study, taking in the cobwebs in every corner and the teetering piles of books, the grate that sat empty, the windowpane that had been cracked for over a decade. He would miss the tidy set of rooms he had shared with Roger. He would miss Roger, full stop. A sick chasm of loss threatened to open inside him. Ash's earliest memory was going to live with Roger as an apprentice engraver; before that was only a series of flickering images, fractured and haunting, scarcely seeming to belong to Ash at all. But from the point he had gone to Roger, he had a home, a name, a place to belong. He had lived with Roger for over fifteen years, first as his apprentice, then as a colleague, always as a friend. A few days earlier, when Roger was preparing to board the ship that would take him to Italy, to a climate more suited to his failing lungs, his parting words had been to advise that Ash stay with the Plums. "Yes, yes, you might well hire a quite respectable set of rooms, but you'll be talking to the shadows and naming every spider and earwig within a week. Stay with the Plums." His mentor had been pale, his voice weak from coughing, his thin gray hair whipping in the wind, so his advice, quite possibly the last words he would speak to Ash in this world, had the weight of a dying request.

"I could still come with you," Ash had said again. He had made this offer so many times it had taken on the cadence of a prayer. "It's not too late." He spoke the words into the wind, to be carried away, off the shores of this island he would never leave.

"I really can't see how you expect me to recover when I'm worried about you," Roger had replied, clasping the younger man's hands. "It's too much to ask."

"It's just seasickness," Ash replied pointlessly, because they both remembered vividly what had happened on the packet to Calais all those years ago, and then on the agonizing return journey to Dover. A storm-tossed ship was a perilous place to have a seizure.

"And I just have a summer cold," Roger had responded. And so Ash had embraced his friend one last time, watched the boat sail away, and then headed for London.

Watching Verity now, as she scribbled on a blotted and crumpled piece of paper, her pale brown hair doing unspeakable things and a vast quantity of ink on her fingers, the grief that had dogged him since Portsmouth started to thin, only to be displaced by something else entirely. She must have encountered a particularly galling turn of phrase in the manuscript she was working on, because she made a strangled sound of outrage as she scribbled it out. How many times had he seen her perform just that movement over the years? He ought to be used to how she affected him, but during the months in Bath—that last, futile effort to see if the waters might restore Roger's health—he must have forgotten how to resist her. He couldn't remember how he used to guard his heart against this sudden rush of fondness.

Without rising to his feet, he reached for an andiron and prodded the fire back to life. He still had on his gloves and coat to ward off the chill, but Verity had doubtless been toiling away in this cold room since breakfast. She occasionally made a sound of approval or a tut of frustration as she turned a page, and her pencil was forever scratching along the manuscript, but otherwise she worked in silence, perfectly still at the desk in the small room above the bookshop that she used as her office. The fire hissed, Ash idly paged through a book he had open on his lap, and Verity worked.

Finally she turned over the last page. "Guess how many times Nate used the word *liberty* in this week's *Register*," she said without looking up from her paper, as if it hadn't been six months since they had last seen one another.

He suppressed a smile and mentally awarded her a point in the game of feigned mutual indifference they had been playing for a decade. He didn't know which of them had started it or why, but he would hardly know how to act if they dropped the pretense.

"Four?" he asked.

"Sixteen!" She put her pen down and looked at him for the first time. There was ink on her cheekbone. "In a single article."

"How tedious of him," Ash remarked lightly. Not for love or money would Ash throw himself between the Plum siblings when they were engaged in one of their skirmishes. Three was a difficult number for friendships, and only by careful neutrality did Ash preserve their balance. "Is it any good?"

"If his goal is to get himself hanged or transported, then yes, I'd say it's quite effective. Sometimes I think he actually wants to get arrested."

Ash thought this was entirely possible. The letters he had received in Bath from friends as well as from Nate and Verity themselves suggested that the arguments between brother and sister on the subject of printing outright seditious libel were escalating even faster than the battles between radicals and the government. "He feels strongly about Pentrich," Ash said, striving for diplomacy.

Verity snorted. "He damned well does feel strongly. And so do I. But I can't see what good his swinging by a rope will do anybody. I daresay this government would be only too glad to see us all dead, then there wouldn't be anybody left to object." She took off her spectacles and rubbed her eyes, smudging ink across her cheek. "He's been saying he wants to travel north for the execution."

Ash frowned. While in Bath, with all his attention on Roger's failing health, he had followed the events in the newspaper as he might the tidings of a far-off land. In Pentrich, Derbyshire, some poor benighted fools, half-mad with hunger and deluded by the lies of a government spy, armed with nothing more than scythes and knives and a harebrained set of demands, had been convicted of high treason. Surrounded by clean white streets and well-fed gentlefolk, the stories coming from the North seemed remote, something that belonged in the past. Roger railed against tyranny until he coughed too hard to speak, while Ash listened with half an ear and reserved his anger for a God who seemed intent on leaving Ash alone in the world.

"The trouble with Nate," Ash said, "is that he's twice as clever as he needs to be."

"You wouldn't think so if you read this article," Verity countered. "He knows I can't manage the press if he goes to prison, and even less if I'm in prison as an accessory." She removed a pin from the knot of hair at the back of her head and used it to fasten a curl that had stubbornly worked its way loose, only succeeding in dislodging two more curls in the process. "At any rate, I altered some of the more incendiary phrases so at least this week's issue won't be the death of us."

She had probably also made her brother's arguments twice as cogent and therefore three times as annoying to the government, but she knew that already. "Let me have a look at it." He reached out and she placed the sheaf of papers in his hand.

Nate's bold scrawl unraveled across the page like a tangled skein of yarn, marked with slashes and arrows, then interwoven with Verity's minuscule copperplate handwriting. Charlie, the Plums' apprentice, would render a fair copy for Verity or Nate to approve before setting type, but Ash had enough practice to decipher Nate's writing without much trouble. He read a few lines and raised an eyebrow. "Mentioning the guillotine was perhaps a bridge too far." Verity had struck that line out with a stroke that nearly pierced the paper.

"You see I'm not exaggerating, then?" she demanded, her eyes bright with the prospect of an argument won.

"Mmm," he murmured, trying to sound noncommittal. But even with Verity's revisions, this article would at the very least bring the *Register* in for a level of scrutiny that would do its publishers no good. The entire country looked like a pot about to boil and Nate was all too eager to throw himself right into the hot water.

She leaned forward and he found himself looking up from the paper expectantly, his own posture mirroring hers. "Heaven help me, I missed you, Ash."

He was taken aback by this foray into earnestness but did his best to hide his surprise behind a mask of cool indifference, quickly refocusing his gaze on the paper. He wanted to tell her that she absolutely needed to stop saying that sort of thing, that he had spent years on the edge of a precipice, and it would take only the slightest breeze to tip him over completely. But he didn't think their friendship could survive that kind of honesty: if they acknowledged the potential he felt between them, then they'd want to do something about it. Then he'd lose her. Ash had endured too many losses, and was not willing to lose either of the Plums. So he leaned back in his chair and raised an eyebrow. "Understandable," he said with a blandness that was only possible after a decade of practice. "Without me around, you'd be the worst radical on the premises."

Verity laughed, a merry gurgle that made Ash's heart almost hurt. "Speak for yourself. I'm an exceptionally good radical. Otherwise I would have let my brother print this bilge unedited even though it would be as good as turning him over to the redcoats. What I meant is that it's reassuring not to be the only one in the house who has second thoughts about giving up one's life and safety for a good cause. You heard that Mr. Hone was arrested?" William Hone, another publisher, had earlier that year spent two months in jail on charges of seditious libel. "He's being treated as a hero. And he is, but I spent the entire summer worried that Nate would be next. I suppose that's selfish, but so be it."

Ash raised an imaginary glass in a toast to the idea of not going to prison. He was not terribly keen on imprisonment himself, being fairly certain a seizure on a stone floor would not be one he would survive.

"How long has it been since the last time you lived with us?" Verity asked, tilting her head and looking at him as if she had just noticed he was there.

"Four years? It was in '13 that Roger and I took the set of rooms near Finsbury Square." They had lodged with the Plums when first coming to London, and then occasionally returned to stay with them in between hired sets of rooms. They had changed residences often, always hoping that it was the damp of a previous lodging that had left Roger in an increasingly worrisome state of health.

"Truly, Ash, I'm glad to have you back," she said, with a frank wistfulness that made Ash's heart thud in his chest. "You've always been a stabilizing influence on Nate."

Ash tried not to be disappointed that Verity had missed him only insofar as his presence helped Nate. She had always thought first of her brother; this was nothing new, although the little worry lines that appeared around her eyes when she spoke of him definitely were.

From beyond the thin sooty window he heard the bells of St. Clement's chime for the second time since he had come in. It was time to leave. He hoisted himself to his feet and looked down at Verity. She was polishing her spectacles on the hem of her shawl; a tumble of tea-brown hair had worked its way loose to fall into her face, and that smudge of ink remained beneath her right eye. She must have sensed him looking at her, because she glanced up. Their gazes caught and lingered a moment too long. Ash promptly rose to his feet and left, closing the door behind him. If he let looks like that happen, they'd all find out exactly how fragile their arrangement was.

How one was meant to feed all these people on a couple of mutton chops Verity did not know. Supper was supposed to serve four: herself, Nate, Ash, and Charlie. But Nate had come home with three friends he met at the pub, which would have been bad enough even if he hadn't evidently also invited Amelia Allenby, the half-grown daughter of Verity's friend. At half past seven, a carriage pulled up in front of the house and disgorged a girl in pearl earbobs and a white muslin frock, dressed as if she were going to dine with the great and good of the land, rather than pick at too few mutton chops and be an eyewitness to sedition. Amelia was seventeen and looked upon Nate with a degree of hero worship that nobody who brought three hungry radicals home to dinner deserved.

Why did it always have to be something like chops when there were unexpected guests? Six days out of seven they had stew of varying consistencies, starting out as something reasonably substantial but stretched and thinned as the week wore on, until it became a sort of watery potato soup. She supposed Nan found a bargain on mutton at the market that morning. At least there were plenty of fresh rolls from the baker. When the dish of mutton was passed around, she handed it to Ash without saying a word. He caught her eye and passed the dish to Amelia on his right without taking any meat for himself.

"Never worry, Plum," he said in a low murmur that made her remember that he was, unfortunately, a man; if she had learned anything in her quarter century in this city it was that men were more trouble than they were worth. "I have a bottle of wine and some cheese upstairs. I'll bring you some later."

"How provident of you," she said, telling herself very firmly that she was not to lean closer to Ash. "Clearly you remember what it takes to survive in this house." The Plums had never kept a decent table, not even in Verity's mother's day, and Verity often wondered that they had any supper guests whatsoever. Not that Ash was a guest; he was, technically, a lodger, which meant he paid for this nipfarthing supper. She sighed. "But I truly can't—"

She was interrupted by raised voices from Nate's end of the table.

"They were sentenced to be hanged, drawn, and quartered. In 1817." Nate smacked his knife down with a thump that shook the table. "Of course I'm outraged. A group of men, after being convicted in a sham trial, are to have the entrails taken out of their still-living bodies. Why wouldn't I be outraged?"

"I don't think it'll come to that," said one of the hearty young men, brandishing an entire mutton chop on the end of his fork. "I don't recall hearing about Despard and his conspirators being disemboweled, although I was only a boy when that happened."

"Drawing doesn't refer to the drawing out of the entrails," said Amelia in her polished and plummy accent, as if this were normal dinner table conversation. Verity noted that the girl had not taken any meat, and appeared to be contenting herself with boiled carrots and a roll. "It refers to the drawing of the convict behind a horse. I was reading about it in a book on the Plantagenets."

"Were all those medieval chaps disemboweled just for fun, then?" the young man asked, leaning across the table towards Amelia. "Just a bit of a flourish on the executioner's behalf, eh?" Verity had the alarming sense that the boy was attempting to flirt with Amelia. Trust one of Nate's friends to flirt by means of discussing capital punishment.

"We're eating," Verity pointed out, knowing it was hopeless. "Maybe we can save the talk of disembowelment for later."

"Or never," Ash suggested. "Never would do."

"You are missing the point," Nate said, entirely ignoring his sister and directly addressing Ash. "For them to be killed at all is barbaric. It's nothing less than murder."

"Of course it's nothing less than murder," Ash said in that deep, steady voice that he had always used to calm Nate down. "It's worse than murder, because it will go unpunished. And of course the trial was grossly wrong and unfair.

We all know that. We all agree at this table." My God, they had been through this often enough in the past months. Verity opened her mouth to say as much but Ash, without looking at her, made a shooing gesture under the table which she interpreted as *Shut up, Plum.* "The only point on which we disagree is whether you're going to print a lunatic screed that gets us all arrested."

"What I wrote is the truth," Nate answered, sounding more like a child of ten than a grown man of past twenty.

"A fat lot of good the truth has ever done anyone," Verity burst out, unable to hold her tongue. "Besides, even the truth can be couched in words that don't get anyone brought before a judge."

"Wooler was acquitted!" Nate protested, referring to a publisher who that summer had been tried for seditious libel after publishing material criticizing the House of Lords. "And I'm certain Hone will be, when he's tried later this autumn."

"And Mr. Cobbett went to America to avoid another turn in prison," she shot back, alluding to a fellow reformer who had once spent two years in prison for a pamphlet that was critical of the government. As soon as Lord Sidmouth ordered the arrest and prosecution of anyone suspected of printing sedition, Cobbett had sailed to New York.

"William Cobbett is an old man," her brother retorted.

"My father says he's done with politics," said one of the young printers, adopting a self-consciously conciliatory tone that made Verity want to crack her dinner plate over his head. "He says he'll only trade in obscenity from now on. Says people will always pay for that, paper duty or no paper duty."

"Less time in prison too," said another man. "And no chance of being done up for treason. Three years hard? Piddling stuff." Verity could not determine whether he was joking.

"Better than transportation or hanging," pointed out the first young man.

"Or disembowelment," agreed the other. They clinked their glasses together in happy salute of the manageable punishment for printing obscenities.

Verity sighed. "I'm so sorry," she told Amelia once the young men had all resumed their quarrel. "They haven't any manners at all."

"This is much more interesting than the dinners I usually attend," she said brightly. Seventeen was young enough for anything to be interesting, Verity supposed.

"I daresay your mother has kept you well clear of sedition and blasphemy. I'll have to apologize to her." Verity groaned inwardly at the prospect. It had been half a year since she and Portia Allenby had ceased being lovers. But they had been friends before, and Portia seemed determined that they would remain friends, even though every moment they spent together reminded Verity of how very ill-suited she was for affection, romance, and possibly even friendship.

Amelia furrowed her brow. "All those scientists she has on her Wednesday nights are quite blasphemous, at least if my understanding of their science and general theology are correct."

Portia Allenby had once been the mistress of a wealthy nobleman and now held a salon at which writers, scientists, and other luminaries gathered. She let her daughters have run of the house no matter what topics were being discussed. But Verity had to think that Portia might not want her eldest daughter to be at a dinner table where there was frank disparagement of the government without the benefit of decent food and wax candles. Good wine helped a great deal to make conversation seem academic rather than something that could at any moment spill out into the streets and end with pitchforks and treason trials.

"Would you ever trade in . . ." Amelia bit her lip, plainly at a loss for words. "In the sort of material the young men were talking about?"

"Lewd novels?" Verity supplied. "Explicit prints? If they were any good, perhaps." Beside her, she heard Ash's low laugh. "Well, I would," she insisted. "We don't put out many books, but I'd make an exception. My father always said that more than one bookseller made his fortune on clandestine printings of *Fanny Hill*. But I wouldn't put out another *Fanny Hill*, which I dare say a number of gentlemen have found very amusing, but it doesn't have much in it for the ladies."

Now she could feel Ash's gaze on her and it gave Verity a strange feeling to be talking about obscene literature so close to him. With so many people crowded around the small table, her shoulder nearly touched his.

"You and your brother are no different," he said, an indulgent half smile playing on his lips. "Any other person would be coming up with law-abiding ways to keep the business afloat. The two of you are fighting over which laws to break."

"If I printed that sort of thing, I'd be most careful, I assure you. Only the best filth for Plum and Company's readership."

Later, after Nate and his friends left to get soused at a gin house and Amelia had been collected by her mother's carriage, Ash and Verity sat amidst the remains of supper and the wine from Ash's room.

"Revolution is all he speaks of," she said while splitting the last roll and giving half to Ash. "And in turn all I talk about is the need for prudence, and so we go round and round. I think we've been having the same conversation since you left for Bath." The wine had gone to her head a bit. Her thoughts were muzzy and her speech was free. "I feel like a prison warden. Or a very cross nursery maid. I'm always scolding Nate or counting farthings or wondering where the last candle went." These repeated quarrels were robbing her of her affection for her brother, the bookshop, and her work. There was so little joy in it, and these days there wasn't even the thrill of working for a good cause, because she felt precious little hope for success in the face of a government bent on tyranny. She drained her glass. "With you here, though, I'm not alone." Good God, she was more than a little drunk if she was being that maudlin out loud.

Ash emptied the wine bottle into her glass. "You've never been alone. You have dozens of people in and out of this house every day—your writers, workers, customers, other booksellers. I've been back less than a day, I haven't left the house, and I've already seen almost everyone I know in this city." The firelight glinted off his dark hair and cast shadows across the strong planes of his face. She hastily looked away.

"That's not what I meant." All those people who came and went wanted or needed something from her. That was the common thread running through every relationship Verity had known, starting with her overbearing father and continuing right through to Portia Allenby. What Verity offered was never enough and now she had nothing left to give. Giving more would mean nothing remained for herself. And maybe that made her hard and unfeeling, but she'd live with that if the alternative was self-effacement.

She felt the warmth of his hand on top of hers and nearly startled in her seat. By unspoken consent, they seldom touched. They had never discussed the parameters of their friendship, but they measured out these touches as carefully as any housewife measured out the lumps in the sugar bowl. They were for special occasions, feast days, homecomings. Two, three touches a year. Any more frequent and heaven knew what would happen.

Verity knew exactly what would happen, though. Sometimes she let herself think of it, when night had fallen and she had the sheets pulled up to her chin. It was important that it never actually come to pass, because Ash was the type who would get ideas and insist on marriage. And the last thing in the world Verity needed was a husband. She had seen what marriage had done to her mother: it had worn her down, whittled her away at the edges until she had all but disappeared. Partly that was because her father had not been a particularly kind man. He had been a radical and a democrat; he had memorized passages from Mary Wollstonecraft's book. But as far as Verity could tell, the man had never once thought to apply those ideas to his own wife. It was, Verity assumed, the old adage about power corrupting: marriage gave a man too much unchecked power over his wife and children, transforming otherwise decent men into petty tyrants. Her mother had ultimately been dependent on the whims of a man who was both mercurial and self-serving, critical and harsh. Verity had fought hard to maintain a degree of control over her fate: Plum and Company was hers as much as it was Nate's, both on paper and as a matter of practical fact. The only people she relied on were those whose wages she paid. The prospect of a husband—and children, presumably—would make that independence impossible.

"Look at me," Ash said, his voice low, and Verity managed to tear her gaze away from where their hands touched. She turned her face up to his. The candles had burnt down and the room was lit only by the fire and one weakly flickering lamp, but she could see the dusting of new beard on his jawline, the dark gleam of his eyes. She allowed herself to appreciate how very handsome he was, another practice she allowed only in the strictest moderation. His hair was nearly black and fell in haphazard waves across his forehead. His jaw was strong but his eyelashes were decadently pretty and he had a few utterly incongruous freckles scattered across his nose. There. She had noticed all those things and still was quite in her right mind.

"Plum," Ash said, and she had the fleeting impression that he was looking at her with the same tightly leashed admiration. He shook his head and let go of her hand. That ought to have been enough to restore their normal equilibrium, but she could still feel the traces of his touch on her. Later, when she was back at her desk, working by the light of a guttering candle, she caught herself wishing that Ash were with her, that his hand was on hers and his body beside hers. She had the uneasy sense that something between them had shifted out of place and she did not know how to put it back the way it belonged.

About the Author

CAT SEBASTIAN lives in a swampy part of the South with her husband, three kids, and two dogs. Before her kids were born, she practiced law and taught high school and college writing. When she isn't reading or writing, she's doing crossword puzzles, bird watching, and wondering where she put her coffee cup.

Discover great authors, exclusive offers, and more at hc.com.